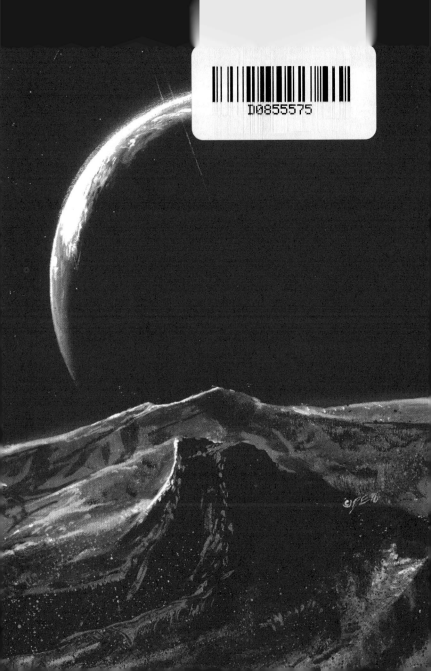

THE Science Fiction COLLECTION BOOK CLUB.

HOME IS THE HANGMAN

ROGER ZELAZNY

Illustrated by Bob Eggleton

First published in *Analog Science Fiction/Science Fact,* November 1975.

Reprinted by permission of
The Pimlico Agency, Inc.
Box 20447
1539 First Avenue
New York, New York 10028

ISBN: 1-56865-227-5

Printed in the United States of America

INTRODUCTION

Roger Zelazny was popular as the creator of the Amber series and admired as a writer of brilliant short fiction, a continuous output over four decades. There are two sequences that make up the Amber fantasy series, the first (five volumes) featuring Corwin and beginning with *Nine Princes in Amber* in 1970 and the second (also five volumes) featuring Corwin's son, Merlin, beginning with *Trumps of Doom* (1985). Zelazny was a great fan of Philip José Farmer and Amber is a new take on Farmer's World of Tiers (a world that is the true reality of which our own is merely a shadow) especially *The Maker of Universes* (1965). The first quintuplet is superior to the second, and is the work that transformed Zelazny's career, made him a bestseller. But it is light entertainment from an accomplished writer with much greater range, depth, and capabilities. In my opinion, his *A Night in the Lonesome October* (1994) is better than any of the Amber books. But his best SF is best of all.

Zelazny arrived like a fire in the sky as an SF writer in 1962. It was the same year that he got his MA in English from Columbia University with an essay on Jacobean Drama. I went and looked it up in 1966 when I was getting a graduate degree there, and the deposit copy if his Masters essay was in the card catalog but was gone from the library, stolen. I found out later that this is common, and it is not unusual for the author to steal it—these things are usually written fast, under pressure, and are not what you want other people reading, and perhaps ridiculing, in later years.

That wonderful year marked not just his advent but that of his contemporaries Ursula K. Le Guin and Thomas M. Disch. All three published many stories in 1962 and 1963 in *Amazing* and *Fantastic*, both edited for that couple of years by Cele Goldsmith—who was the first woman editor to win a Hugo Award—and then went on in the mid-60s to publish novels of extraordinarily high achievement with Ace Books. With R. A. Lafferty, Joanna Russ, Norman Spinrad, Samuel R. Delany, Larry Niven, and Anne McCaffrey, they were the hot new writers of the sixties.

But Zelazny was the leader of them all in immediate popular success. His first novel, *This Immortal*, won the 1966 Hugo Award in a tie with Frank Herbert's *Dune*. His "He Who Shapes," won the 1965 Nebula for best novella in 1966, while his "The Doors of his Face, the Lamps of his Mouth" won the Nebula for best novelette. And that popularity was wedded to critical acclaim too. His sophisticated language and gracefully ornamented style, which still retained precision and clarity, raised the literary stakes for SF, and he, leading the

iii

younger writers mentioned, seemed for a few years about to catapult the whole SF field onto a new level of achievement.

My first encounter with Zelazny's fiction was the novella, "A Rose for Ecclesiastes" (1963) in *The Magazine of Fantasy & Science Fiction*, the cover story of the issue, with a glorious and colorful wraparound cover that was the last major work of the great fantasy artist Hannes Bok. That story was immediately evident as a new classic in the SF tradition of Mars stories set on a Mars not of contemporary scientific accuracy but of the SF imagination: the Mars tradition of Burroughs and Bradbury, of Brackett and Ballard. I became at that instant an admirer. He once said in my hearing to Brian W. Aldiss that Aldiss' story about a man fleeing from loving his mother, "A Kind of Artistry" (1962), was the breakthrough piece that showed him the way to write ambitious SF. The intense dramatization in the external world of inner psychological states colorfully transformed in an SF setting was there. I could see it, but it also struck me that his early fiction might owe something to "The Blind Pilot," a story by Nathalie and Charles Henneberg translated from the French by Damon Knight that appeared in 1960 in *F&SF*, that shared the fascination evident in Aldiss with doomed, myth-haunted, heroic characters and image-laden prose, with projections of the psyche in SF settings.

Samuel R. Delany, the writer whose reputation most matched Zelazny's in the 1960s, has often referred to "the ten novellas of the sixties" as Zelazny's most important body of major work, comparable in impact on SF writers and readers to the 13 stories Alfred Bester published in the 1950s. While novels such as the Hugo-winning *Lord of Light* (1968) might appear disproportionally important in the history books, it was the long stories such as the three named above and "The Keys to December," "The Graveyard Heart," "For a Breath I Tarry," and "Damnation Alley" that electrified the field. What those stories did was to show everyone that there was new, more ambitious ways to view and to treat the old settings of science fiction. This may seem a simple idea in retrospect, but radical transformation is often based on a simple shift of paradigms. It worked then, for Zelazny and his generation of peers. It helped by example to jump-start the idling literary engines of a number of already-established SF writers, from Clifford D. Simak to Robert Silverberg. Zelazny was more than a writer—he was a symbol of change.

This evidently put more pressure on him than he wished to bear. He ignored his symbolic status and in 1968 and 69 he took advantage of the commercial potential of his public acclaim and began to branch out all over the lot. He signed contracts with several publishers, wrote fast, and made money at a time when writing a lot of books was the only way to make money in SF. The highest single paperback advance ever paid to a science fiction writer as of 1972 was $10,000.00, and it had not been to Zelazny. Everyone in the early 1970s was paid around the same price, $5000.00, for a novel, and no one would have wished to try to live on that—so everyone tried to write more. Zelazny even wrote "extra" novels in collaboration with Philip K. Dick and Fred Saberhagen.

He was prolific throughout the 1970s, gaining in mass appeal, and finally relatively well-off from the proceeds of the Amber books. But to some of his early fans and to some SF critics he was a fallen idol after 1970. Some of them were mean to him in print, some even in person. They kept examining each new novel for signs of the return of the king of literary SF, and not finding any—or too few to satisfy them. I worked occasionally with him from 1970 until the 1990s and observed that his need (or desire) to make more money often kept him from working on projects in the 1970s and 1980s that were more speculative financially than another Amber book. Of course from the mid-70s onward, any Amber project paid bigger. So he allowed himself free rein on his literary ambition only in pieces shorter than novel length.

His career lasted for over thirty years and although he changed his ambitions at the end of the 1960s and adopted something of a different writerly stance in the 1970s and for the rest of his writing lifetime, he always maintained his ability to craft effective short fiction, especially at novella length, as fine as any written in the field. "Home is the Hangman," a novella that won the Hugo and the Nebula in 1976, is only one of a number of pieces that showed his mastery over three decades. It was the third of three pieces (the other two are "The Eve of Rumoko" and "Kjwalll'kje'k'koothaill'kje'k") combined to form the volume *My Name is Legion* (1976).

All three stories feature the same central character, a nameless freelance operative who lives in the 21st century U.S.A. Once he was a computer scientist who worked on the great central data bank that now contains everyone's records—but he deleted his own and became free and utterly anonymous. In each story he hires himself out to assist private detective Don Walsh on top secret cases. Roger Zelazny was a great fan of the hard-boiled mystery genre (Corwin of Amber in *Nine Princes*) speaks just like the classic hard-boiled detective and his problem-solving heroes often unravel mysteries. Here, in "Home is the Hangman," we have several levels of mystery, as well as an overt investigation that goes shockingly awry—and very cleverly. What impresses me most about Zelazny in this story is the extent to which he can entertain with wit and charm while giving really quite large chunks of precise and difficult exposition about society and computers, robots, space exploration, artificial intelligence, and a variety of social issues—there is a lot of knowledge and science in this fiction. What also impresses me is his clever plotting and pacing that give the illusion of action to what is essentially science fiction in the tradition of Asimov and Heinlein—a series of descriptions and conversations. Most of the action is in your head.

Personally, I am left with many images of the gentleman who wrote this fascinating work. Roger was quite tall, thin, lantern-jawed, a bit hunched over, with a deep, powerful voice he could use for public readings (and he could "do voices"). He could make wonderful cat's cradles of string. He studied martial arts. He collected comics—he owned a first issue of Superman, I believe. I once heard him say that he had as a student read Northrup Frye's *Anatomy of Criticism* and decided that he would write in the mythic heroic mode in part because it was so little used today by serious writers. Perhaps that was partly a joke on the academics present when he said it—probably comic books and old SF magazines influenced him as strongly toward the heroic. And maybe Jacobean drama, too—one tends to forget how extraordinarily heroic, as well as violent, horrific, and twisted that dramatic era was. In some ways he was a younger version of Fritz Leiber. And before he died he worked as hard as he ever had at the challenge of completing the draft of a novel Alfred Bester had left unfinished. What he worked to attain was an honorable emulation of Bester's pyrotechnic style—which he did accomplish. In the end he was himself, in love with what he did so well, writing.

—David G. Hartwell
Pleasantville, N.Y.

HOME IS THE
HANGMAN

Big fat flakes down the night, silent night, windless night. And I never count them as storms unless there is wind. Not a sigh or a whimper, though. Just a cold, steady whiteness, drifting down outside the window, and a silence confirmed by gunfire, driven deeper now it had ceased. In the main room of the lodge the only sounds were the occasional hiss and sputter of the logs turning to ashes on the grate.

I sat in a chair turned sidewise from the table to face the door. A tool kit rested on the floor to my left. The helmet stood on the table, a lopsided basket of metal, quartz, porcelain, and glass. If I heard the click of a microswitch followed by a humming sound from within it, then a faint light would come on beneath the meshing near to its forward edge and begin to blink rapidly. If these things occurred, there was a very strong possibility that I was going to die.

I had removed a black ball from my pocket

1

when Larry and Bert had gone outside, armed, respectively, with a flame thrower and what looked like an elephant gun. Bert had also taken two grenades with him.

I unrolled the black ball, opening it out into a seamless glove, a dollop of something resembling moist putty stuck to its palm. Then I drew the glove on over my left hand and sat with it upraised, elbow resting on the arm of the chair. A small laser flash pistol in which I had very little faith lay beside my right hand on the table-top, next to the helmet.

If I were to slap a metal surface with my left hand, the substance would adhere there, coming free of the glove. Two seconds later it would explode, and the force of the explosion would be directed in against the surface. Newton would claim his own by way of right-angled redistributions of the reaction, hopefully tearing lateral hell out of the contact surface. A smother-charge, it was called, and its posses-

2

sion came under concealed weapons and possession of burglary tools statutes in most places. The molecularly gimmicked goo, I decided, was great stuff. It was just the delivery system that left more to be desired.

Beside the helmet, next to the gun, in front of my hand, stood a small walkie-talkie. This was for purposes of warning Bert and Larry if I should hear the click of a microswitch followed by a humming sound, should see a light come on and begin to blink rapidly. Then they would know that Tom and Clay, with whom we had lost contact when the shooting began, had failed to destroy the enemy and doubtless lay lifeless at their stations now, a little over a kilometer to the south. Then they would know that they, too, were probably about to die.

I called out to them when I heard the click. I picked up the helmet and rose to my feet as its light began to blink.

But it was already too late.

3

The fourth place listed on the Christmas card I had sent Don Walsh the previous year was Peabody's Book Shop and Beer Stube in Baltimore, Maryland. Accordingly, on the last night in October I sat in its rearmost room, at the final table before the alcove with the door leading to the alley. Across that dim chamber, a woman dressed in black played the ancient upright piano, up-tempoing everything she touched. Off to my right, a fire wheezed and spewed fumes on a narrow hearth beneath a crowded mantelpiece overseen by an ancient and antlered profile. I sipped a beer and listened to the sounds.

I half hoped that this would be one of the occasions when Don failed to show up. I had sufficient funds to hold me through spring and I did not really feel like working. I had summered farther north, was anchored now in the Chesapeake, and was anxious to continue Ca-

4

ribbeanwards. A growing chill and some nasty winds told me I had tarried overlong in these latitudes. Still, the understanding was that I remain in the chosen bar until midnight. Two hours to go.

I ate a sandwich and ordered another beer. About halfway into it, I spotted Don approaching the entranceway, topcoat over his arm, head turning. I manufactured a matching quantity of surprise when he appeared beside my table with a "Ron! Is that really you?"

I rose and clasped his hand.

"Alan! Small world, or something like that. Sit down! Sit down!"

He settled onto the chair across from me, draped his coat over the one to his left.

"What are you doing in this town?" he asked.

"Just a visit," I answered. "Said hello to a few friends." I patted the scars, the stains of the venerable surface before me. "And this is my last stop. I'll be leaving in a few hours."

5

He chuckled.

"Why is it that you knock on wood?"

I grinned.

"I was expressing affection for one of Henry Mencken's favorite speakeasies."

"This place dates back that far?"

I nodded.

"It figures," he said. "You've got this thing for the past—or against the present. I'm never sure which."

"Maybe a little of both," I said. "I wish Mencken would stop in. I'd like his opinion on the present. What are you doing with it?"

"What?"

"The present. Here. Now."

"Oh." He spotted the waitress and ordered a beer. "Business trip," he said then. "To hire a consultant."

"Oh. And how *is* business?"

"Complicated," he said, "complicated."

We lit cigarettes and after a while his beer

6

arrived. We smoked and drank and listened to the music.

I've sung this song and I'll sing it again: the world is like an uptempoed piece of music. Of the many changes which came to pass during my lifetime, it seems that the majority have occurred during the past few years. It also struck me that way several years ago, and I'd a hunch I might be feeling the same way a few years hence—that is, if Don's business did not complicate me off this mortal coil or condenser before then.

Don operates the second-largest detective agency in the world, and he sometimes finds me useful because I do not exist. I do not exist now because I existed once at the time and the place where we attempted to begin scoring the wild ditty of our times. I refer to the World Data Bank project and the fact that I had had a significant part in that effort to construct a working model of the real world, accounting for

7

everyone and everything in it. How well we suc-
ceeded and whether possession of the world's
likeness does indeed provide its custodians with
a greater measure of control over its functions
are questions my former colleagues still debate
as the music grows more shrill and you can't see
the maps for the pins. I made my decision back
then and saw to it that I did not receive citizen-
ship in that second world, a place which may
now have become more important than the
first. Exiled to reality, my own sojourns across
the line are necessarily those of an alien guilty
of illegal entry. I visit periodically because I go
where I must to make my living. That is where
Don comes in. The people I can become are often very useful when he has peculiar problems.
Unfortunately, at that moment, it seemed that
he did, just when the whole gang of me felt like
turning down the volume and loafing.

We finished our drinks, got the bill, settled
it.

8

"This way," I said, indicating the rear door, and he swung into his coat and followed me out.

"Talk here?" he asked, as we walked down the alley.

"Rather not," I said. "Public transportation, then private conversation."

He nodded and came along.

About three-quarters of an hour later we were in the saloon of the *Proteus* and I was making coffee. We were rocked gently by the Bay's chill waters, under a moonless sky. I'd only a pair of the smaller lights burning. Comfortable. On the water, aboard the *Proteus,* the crowding, the activities, the tempo, of life in the cities, on the land, are muted, slowed—fictionalized—by the metaphysical distancing a few meters of water can provide. We alter the landscape with great facility, but the ocean has always seemed unchanged, and I suppose by extension we are infected with some feelings of

9

timelessness whenever we set out upon her. Maybe that's one of the reasons I spend so much time there.

"First time you've had me aboard," he said. "Comfortable. Very."

"Thanks. Cream? Sugar?"

"Yes. Both."

We settled back with our steaming mugs and I said, "What have you got?"

"One case involving two problems," he said. "One of them sort of falls within my area of competence. The other does not. I was told that it is an absolutely unique situation and would require the services of a very special specialist."

"I'm not a specialist at anything but keeping alive."

His eyes came up suddenly and caught my own.

"I had always assumed that you knew an awful lot about computers," he said.

I looked away. That was hitting below the

belt. I had never held myself out to him as an authority in that area, and there had always been a tacit understanding between us that my methods of manipulating circumstance and identity were not open to discussion. On the other hand, it was obvious to him that my knowledge of the system was both extensive and intensive. Still, I didn't like talking about it. So I moved to defend.

"Computer people are a dime a dozen," I said. "It was probably different in your time, but these days they start teaching computer science to little kids their first year in school. So, sure I know a lot about it. This generation, everybody does."

"You know that is not what I meant," he said. "Haven't you known me long enough to trust me a little more than that? The question springs solely from the case at hand. That's all."

I nodded. Reactions by their very nature are not always appropriate, and I had invested a lot

11

of emotional capital in a heavy-duty set. So, "O.K., I know more about them than the school kids," I said.

"Thanks. That can be our point of departure." He took a sip of coffee. "My own background is in law and accounting, followed by the military, military intelligence, and civil service, in that order. Then I got into this business. What technical stuff I know I've picked up along the way, a scrap here, a crash course there. I know a lot about what things can do, not so much about how they work. I did not understand the details on this one, so I want you to start at the top and explain things to me, for as far as you can go. I need the background review, and if you are able to furnish it I will also know that you are the man for the job. You can begin by telling me how the early space exploration robots worked—like, say, the ones they used on Venus."

"That's not computers," I said, "and for that

12

matter, they weren't really robots. They were telefactoring devices."

"Tell me what makes the difference."

"A robot is a machine which carries out certain operations in accordance with a program of instructions. A telefactor is a slave machine operated by remote control. The telefactor functions in a feedback situation with its operator. Depending on how sophisticated you want to get, the links can be audiovisual, kinesthetic, tactile, even olfactory. The more you want to go in this direction, the more anthropomorphic you get in the thing's design. In the case of Venus, if I recall correctly, the human operator in orbit wore an exoskeleton which controlled the movements of the body, legs, arms, and hands of the device on the surface below, receiving motion and force feedback through a system of airjet transducers. He had on a helmet controlling the slave device's television camera—set, obviously enough, in its turret—

13

which filled his field of vision with the scene below. He also wore earphones connected with its audio pickup. I read the book he wrote later. He said that for long stretches of time, he would forget the cabin, forget that he was at the boss end of a control loop and actually feel as if he were stalking through that hellish landscape. I remember being very impressed by it, just being a kid, and I wanted a super-tiny one all my own, so that I could wade around in puddles picking fights with microorganisms."

"Why?"

"Because there weren't any dragons on Venus. Anyhow, that is a telefactoring device, a thing quite distinct from a robot."

"I'm still with you," he said. "Now tell me the difference between the early telefactoring devices and the later ones."

I swallowed some coffee.

"It was a bit trickier with respect to the outer planets and their satellites," I said.

14

"There, we did not have orbiting operators at first. Economics, and some unresolved technical problems. Mainly economics. At any rate, the devices were landed on the target worlds, but the operators stayed home. Because of this, there was of course a time lag in the transmissions along the control loop. It took a while to receive the onsite input, and then there was another time lapse before the response movements reached the telefactor. We attempted to compensate for this in two ways. The first was by the employment of a simple wait-move, wait-move sequence. The second was more sophisticated and is actually the point where computers come into the picture in terms of participating in the control loop. It involved the setting up of models of known environmental factors, which were then enriched during the initial wait-move sequences. On this basis, the computer was then used to anticipate short-range developments. Finally, it could take over the loop and

15

run it by a combination of 'predictor controls' and wait-move reviews. It still had to holler for human help, though, when unexpected things came up. So, with the outer planets, it was neither totally automatic nor totally manual—nor totally satisfactory—at first."

"O.K.," he said, lighting a cigarette. "And the next step?"

"The next wasn't really a technical step forward in telefactoring. It was an economic shift. The purse strings were loosened and we could afford to send men out. We landed them where we could land them, and in many of the places where we could not we sent down the telefactors and orbited the men again. Like in the old days. The time lag problem was removed because the operator was on top of things once more. If anything, you can look at it as a reversion to earlier methods. It is what we still often do, though, and it works."

He shook his head.

16

"You left something out," he said, "between the computers and the bigger budget."

I shrugged.

"A number of things were tried during that period," I said, "but none of them proved as effective as what we already had going in the human-computer partnership with the telefactors."

"There was one project," he said, "which attempted to get around the time lag troubles by sending the computer along with the telefactor as part of the package. Only the computer wasn't exactly a computer and the telefactor wasn't exactly a telefactor. Do you know which one I am referring to?"

I lit a cigarette of my own while I thought about it, then "I think you are talking about the Hangman," I said.

"That's right," he said, "and this is where I get lost. Can you tell me how it works?"

"Ultimately, it was a failure," I said.

17

"But it worked at first."

"Apparently. But only on the easy stuff, on Io. It conked out later and had to be written off as a failure, albeit a noble one. The venture was overly ambitious from the very beginning. What seems to have happened was that the people in charge had the opportunity to combine vanguard projects—stuff that was still under investigation and stuff that was extremely new. In theory it all seemed to dovetail so beautifully that they yielded to the temptation and incorporated too much. It started out well, but it fell apart later."

"But what all was involved in the thing?"

"Lord! What wasn't? The computer that wasn't exactly a computer . . . O.K., we'll start there. Last century, three engineers at the University of Wisconsin—Nordman, Parmentier, and Scott—developed a device known as a superconductive tunnel junction neuristor. Two tiny strips of metal with a thin insulating

18

layer between. Supercool it and it passed electrical impulses without resistance. Surround it with magnetized material and pack a mass of them together—billions—and what have you got?"

He shook his head.

"Well, for one thing you've got an impossible situation to schematize when considering all the paths and interconnections that may be formed. There is an obvious similarity to the structure of the brain. So, they theorized, you don't even attempt to hook up such a device. You pulse in data and let it establish its own preferential pathways, by means of the magnetic material's becoming increasingly magnetized each time the current passes through it, thus cutting the resistance. So the material establishes its own routes in a fashion analogous to the functioning of the brain when it is learning something. In the case of the Hangman, they used a setup very similar to this and they

19

were able to pack over ten billion neuristor-type cells into a very small area—around a cubic foot. They aimed for that magic figure because that is approximately the number of nerve cells in the human brain. That is what I meant when I said that it wasn't really a computer. They were actually working in the area of artificial intelligence, no matter what they called it."

"If the thing had its own brain—computer or quasi-human—then it was a robot rather than a telefactor, right?"

"Yes and no and maybe," I said. "It was operated as a telefactor device here on Earth—on the ocean floor, in the desert, in mountainous country—as part of its programming. I suppose you could also call that its apprenticeship or kindergarten. Perhaps that is even more appropriate. It was being shown how to explore in difficult environments and to report back. Once it mastered this, then theoretically they could

20

hang it out there in the sky without a control loop and let it report its own findings."

"At that point would it be considered a robot?"

"A robot is a machine which carries out certain operations in accordance with a program of instructions. The Hangman made its own decisions, you see. And I suspect that by trying to produce something that close to the human brain in structure and function the seemingly inevitable randomness of its model got included in. It wasn't just a machine following a program. It was too complex. That was probably what broke it down."

Don chuckled.

"Inevitable free will?"

"No. As I said, they had thrown too many things into one bag. Everybody and his brother with a pet project that might be fitted in seemed a supersalesman that season. For example, the psychophysics boys had a gimmick

21

they wanted to try on it, and it got used. Ostensibly, it was a communications device. Actually, they were concerned as to whether the thing was truly sentient."

"Was it?"

"Apparently so, in a limited fashion. What they had come up with, to be made part of the initial telefactor loop, was a device which set up a weak induction field in the brain of the operator. The machine received and amplified the patterns of electrical activity being conducted in the Hangman's—might as well call it 'brain'—then passed them through a complex modulator and pulsed them into the induction field in the operator's head. I am out of my area now and into that of Weber and Fechner, but a neuron has a threshold at which it will fire, and below which it will not. There are some forty thousand neurons packed together in a square millimeter of the cerebral cortex, in such a fashion that each one has sev-

22

eral hundred synaptic connections with others about it. At any given moment, some of them may be way below the firing threshold while others are in a condition Sir John Eccles once referred to as 'critically poised'—ready to fire. If just one is pushed over the threshold, it can affect the discharge of hundreds of thousands of others within twenty milliseconds. The pulsating field was to provide such a push in a sufficiently selective fashion to give the operator an idea as to what was going on in the Hangman's brain. And vice versa. The Hangman was to have its own built-in version of the same thing. It was also thought that this might serve to humanize it somewhat, so that it would better appreciate the significance of its work—to instill something like loyalty, you might say."

"Do you think this could have contributed to its later breakdown?"

"Possibly. How can you say in a one-of-a-kind situation like this? If you want a guess, I'd say yes. But it's just a guess."

"Uh-huh," he said, "and what were its physical capabilities?"

"Anthropomorphic design," I said, "both because it was originally telefactored and because of the psychological reasoning I just mentioned. It could pilot its own small vessel. No need for a life-support system, of course. Both it and the vessel were powered by fusion units, so that fuel was no real problem. Self-repairing. Capable of performing a great variety of sophisticated tests and measurements, of making observations, completing reports, learning new material, broadcasting its findings back here. Capable of surviving just about anywhere. In fact, it required less energy on the outer planets—less work for the refrigeration units, to maintain that supercooled brain in its midsection."

"How strong was it?"

"I don't recall all the specs. Maybe a dozen

24

times as strong as a man, in things like lifting and pushing."

"It explored Io for us and started in on Europa."

"Yes."

"Then it began behaving erratically, just when we thought it had really learned its job."

"That sounds right," I said.

"It refused a direct order to explore Callisto, then headed out toward Uranus."

"Yes. It's been years since I read the reports. . . ."

"The malfunction worsened after that. Long periods of silence interspersed with garbled transmissions. Now that I know more about its makeup, it almost sounds like a man going off the deep end."

"It seems similar."

"But it managed to pull itself together again for a brief while. It landed on Titania, began sending back what seemed like appropriate ob-

25

servation reports. This only lasted a short time, though. It went irrational once more, indicated that it was heading for a landing on Uranus itself, and that was it. We didn't hear from it after that. Now that I know about that mind-reading gadget I understand why a psychiatrist on this end could be so positive it would never function again."

"I never heard about that part."

"I did."

I shrugged.

"This was all around twenty years ago," I said, "and, as I mentioned, it has been a long while since I've read anything about it."

"The Hangman's ship crashed or landed, as the case may be, in the Gulf of Mexico," he said, "two days ago."

I just stared at him.

"It was empty," he said, "when they finally got out and down to it."

"I don't understand."

26

"Yesterday morning," he went on, "restaurateur Manny Burns was found beaten to death in the office of his establishment, the Maison Saint-Michel, in New Orleans."

"I still fail to see . . ."

"Manny Burns was one of the four original operators who programmed—pardon me, 'taught'—the Hangman."

The silence lengthened, dragged its belly on the deck.

"Coincidence . . . ?" I finally said.

"My client doesn't think so."

"Who is your client?"

"One of the three remaining members of the training group. He is convinced that the Hangman has returned to Earth to kill its former operators."

"Has he made his fears known to his old employers?"

"No."

"Why not?"

27

"Because it would require telling them the reason for his fears."

"That being . . . ?"

"He wouldn't tell me either."

"How does he expect you to do a proper job?"

"He told me what he considered a proper job. He wants two things done, neither of which requires a full case history. He wanted to be furnished with good bodyguards, and he wanted the Hangman found and disposed of. I have already taken care of the first part."

"And you want me to do the second?"

"That's right. You have confirmed my opinion that you are the man for the job."

"I see," I said. "Do you realize that if the thing is truly sentient this will be something very like murder? If it is not, of course, then it will only amount to the destruction of expensive government property."

"Which way do you look at it?"

28

"I look at it as a job," I said.

"You'll take it?"

"I need more facts before I can decide. Like . . . Who is your client? Who are the other operators? Where do they live? What do they do? What—"

He raised his hand.

"First," he said, "the Honorable Jesse Brockden, senior senator from Wisconsin, is our client. Confidentiality, of course, is written all over it."

I nodded.

"I remember his being involved with the space program before he went into politics. I wasn't aware of the specifics, though. He could get government protection so easily—"

"To obtain it, he would apparently have to tell them something he doesn't want to talk about. Perhaps it would hurt his career. I simply do not know. He doesn't want them. He wants us."

I nodded again.

"What about the others? Do they want us, too?"

"Quite the opposite. They don't subscribe to Brockden's notions at all. They seem to think he is something of a paranoid."

"How well do they know one another these days?"

"They live in different parts of the country, haven't seen each other in years. Been in occasional touch, though."

"Kind of flimsy basis for that diagnosis, then."

"One of them *is* a psychiatrist."

"Oh. Which one?"

"Leila Thackery is her name. Lives in St. Louis. Works at the State Hospital there."

"None of them have gone to any authority, then—federal or local?"

"That's right. Brockden contacted them when he heard about the Hangman. He was in Washington at the time. Got word on its return

30

right away and managed to get the story killed. He tried to reach them all, learned about Burns in the process, contacted me, then tried to persuade the others to accept protection by my people. They weren't buying. When I talked to her, Dr. Thackery pointed out—quite correctly—that Brockden is a very sick man—"

"What's he got?"

"Cancer. In his spine. Nothing they can do about it once it hits there and digs in. He even told me he figures he has maybe six months to get through what he considers a very important piece of legislation—the new criminal rehabilitation act. I will admit that he did sound kind of paranoid when he talked about it. But hell! Who wouldn't? Dr. Thackery sees that as the whole thing, though, and she doesn't see the Burns killing as being connected with the Hangman. Thinks it was just a traditional robbery gone sour, thief surprised and panicky, maybe hopped up, et cetera."

31

"Then she is not afraid of the Hangman?"

"She said that she is in a better position to know its mind than anyone else, and she is not especially concerned."

"What about the other operator?"

"He said that Dr. Thackery may know its mind better than anyone else, but he knows its brain, and he isn't worried either."

"What did he mean by that?"

"David Fentris is a consulting engineer—electronics, cybernetics. He actually had something to do with the Hangman's design."

I got to my feet and went after the coffee pot. Not that I'd an overwhelming desire for another cup at just that moment. But I had known, had once worked with a David Fentris. And he had at one time been connected with the space program.

About fifteen years my senior, Dave had been with the Data Bank project when I had known him. Where a number of us had begun having second thoughts as the thing progressed, Dave had never been anything less than wildly enthusiastic. A wiry five-eight, white-cropped, gray eyes back of hornrims and heavy glass, cycling between preoccupation and near-frantic darting, he had had a way of verbalizing half-completed thoughts as he went along, so that you might begin to think him a representative of that tribe which had come into positions of small authority by means of nepotism or politics. If you would listen a few more minutes, though, you would begin revising your opinion as he started to pull his musings together into a rigorous framework. By the time he had finished you generally wondered why you hadn't seen it all along and what a guy like that was doing in a position of such small authority. Later, it might strike you, though, that he seemed sad whenever he wasn't enthusiastic about something, and while the gung-ho spirit is great for short-range projects, larger ventures generally

33

require something more of equanimity. I wasn't at all surprised that he had wound up as a consultant. The big question now, of course, was would he remember me? True, my appearance was altered, my personality hopefully more mature, my habits shifted around. But would that be enough, should I have to encounter him as part of this job? That mind behind those horn-rims could do a lot of strange things with just a little data.

"Where does he live?" I asked.

"Memphis, and what's the matter?"

"Just trying to get my geography straight," I said. "Is Senator Brockden still in Washington?"

"No. He's returned to Wisconsin and is currently holed up in a lodge in the northern part of the state. Four of my people are with him."

"I see."

I refreshed our coffee supply and reseated myself. I didn't like this one at all and I resolved

34

not to take it. I didn't like just giving Don a flat no, though. His assignments had become a very important part of my life, and this one was not mere legwork. It was obviously important to him, and he wanted me on it. I decided to look for holes in the thing, to find some way of reducing it to the simple bodyguard job already in progress.

"It does seem peculiar," I said, "that Brockden is the only one afraid of the device."

"Yes."

". . . And that he gives no reasons."

"True."

". . . Plus his condition, and what the doctor said about its effect on his mind."

"I have no doubt that he is neurotic," Don said. "Look at this."

He reached for his coat, withdrew a sheaf of papers from within it. He shuffled through them and extracted a single sheet, which he passed to me. It was a piece of congressional

35

letterhead stationery, with the message scrawled in longhand: "Don," it said, "I've got to see you. Frankenstein's monster has just come back from where we hung him and he's looking for me. The whole damn universe is trying to grind me up. Call me between eight and ten. —Jess." I nodded, started to pass it back, paused, then handed it over. Double damn it deeper than hell! I took a drink of coffee. I thought that I had long ago given up hope in such things, but I had noticed something which immediately troubled me. In the margin where they list such matters, I had seen that Jesse Brockden was on the committee for review of the Data Bank program. I recalled that that committee was supposed to be working on a series of reform recommendations. Offhand, I could not remember Brockden's position on any of the issues involved, but—oh hell! The thing was simply too big to alter significantly now. . . . But it *was* the only real

36

Frankenstein monster I cared about, and there was always the possibility.... On the other hand—hell, again. What if I let him die when I might have saved him, and he had been the one who...?

I took another drink of coffee. I lit another cigarette. There might be a way of working it so that Dave didn't even come into the picture. I could talk to Leila Thackery first, check further into the Burns killing, keep posted on new developments, find out more about the vessel in the Gulf.... I might be able to accomplish something, even if it was only the negation of Brockden's theory, without Dave's and my paths ever crossing.

"Have you got the specs on the Hangman?" I asked.

"Right here."

He passed them over.

"The police report on the Burns killing?"

"Here it is."

"The whereabouts of everyone involved, and some background on them?"

"Here."

"The place or places where I can reach you during the next few days—around the clock? This one may require some coordination."

He smiled and reached for his pen.

"Glad to have you aboard," he said.

I reached over and tapped the barometer. I shook my head.

The ringing of the phone awakened me. Reflex bore me across the room, where I took it on audio.

"Yes?"

"Mr. Donne? It is eight o'clock."

"Thanks."

I collapsed into the chair. I am what might be called a slow starter. I tend to recapitulate phylogeny every morning. Basic desires inched their ways through my gray matter to close a connection. Slowly, I extended a cold-blooded member and clicked my talons against a couple numbers. I croaked my desire for food and lots of coffee to the voice that responded. Half an hour later I would only have growled. Then I staggered off to the place of flowing waters to renew my contact with basics.

In addition to my normal adrenaline and blood-sugar bearishness, I had not slept much the night before. I had closed up shop after Don had left, stuffed my pockets with essentials, departed the *Proteus,* gotten myself over to the airport and onto a flight which took me to St. Louis in the dead, small hours of the dark. I was unable to sleep during the flight, thinking about the case, deciding on the tack I was going to take with Leila Thackery. On arrival, I had checked into the airport motel, left a message to be awakened at an unreasonable hour, and collapsed.

As I ate, I regarded the fact sheet Don had

39

given me: Leila Thackery was currently single, having divorced her second husband a little over two years ago, was forty-six years old, and lived in an apartment near to the hospital where she worked. Attached to the sheet was a photo which might have been ten years old. In it, she was brunette, light-eyed, barely on the right side of that border between ample and overweight, with fancy glasses straddling an upturned nose. She had published a number of books and articles with titles full of alienations, roles, transactions, social contexts, and more alienations.

I hadn't had the time to go my usual route, becoming an entire new individual with a verifiable history. Just a name and a story, that's all. It did not seem necessary this time, though. For once, something approximating honesty actually seemed a reasonable approach.

I took a public vehicle over to her apartment building. I did not phone ahead, because it is easier to say no to a voice than to a person.

According to the record, today was one of the days when she saw outpatients in her home. Her idea, apparently: break down the alienating institution image, remove resentments by turning the sessions into something more like social occasions, et cetera. I did not want all that much of her time, I had decided that Don could make it worth her while if it came to that, and I was sure my fellows' visits were scheduled to leave her with some small breathing space— *inter alia,* so to speak.

I had just located her name and apartment number amid the buttons in the entrance foyer when an old woman passed behind me and unlocked the door to the lobby. She glanced at me and held it open, so I went on in without ringing. The matter of presence, again.

I took the elevator to Leila's floor, the second. I located her door and knocked on it. I was almost ready to knock again when it opened, partway.

41

"Yes?" she asked, and I revised my estimate as to the age of the photo. She looked just about the same.

"Dr. Thackery," I said, "my name is Donne. You could help me quite a bit with a problem I've got."

"What sort of problem?"

"It involves a device known as the Hangman."

She sighed and showed me a quick grimace. Her fingers tightened on the door.

"I've come a long way but I'll be easy to get rid of. I've only a few things I'd like to ask you about it."

"Are you with the government?"

"No."

"Do you work for Brockden?"

"No. I'm something different."

"All right," she said. "Right now I've got a group session going. It will probably last around another half hour. If you don't mind waiting down in the lobby, I'll let you know as soon as it is over. We can talk then."

"Good enough," I said. "Thanks."

She nodded, closed the door. I located the stairway and walked back down.

A cigarette later, I decided that the devil finds work for idle hands and thanked him for his suggestion. I strolled back toward the foyer. Through the glass, I read the names of a few residents of the fifth floor. I elevated up and knocked on one of the doors. Before it was opened I had my notebook and pad in plain sight.

"Yes?"—short, fiftyish, curious.

"My name is Stephen Foster, Mrs. Gluntz. I am doing a survey for the North American Consumers' League. I would like to pay you for a couple minutes of your time, to answer some questions about products you use."

"Why . . . pay me?"

"Yes, ma'am. Ten dollars. Around a dozen questions. It will just take a minute or two."

43

"All right." She opened the door wider. "Won't you come in?"

"No, thank you. This thing is so brief I'd just be in and out. The first question involves detergents—"

Ten minutes later I was back in the lobby adding the thirty bucks for the three interviews to the list of expenses I was keeping. When a situation is full of unpredictables and I am playing makeshift games, I like to provide for as many contingencies as I can.

Another quarter of an hour or so slipped by before the elevator opened and discharged three guys, young, young, and middle-aged, casually dressed, chuckling over something. The big one on the nearest end strolled over and nodded.

"You the fellow waiting to see Dr. Thackery?"

"That's right."

"She said to tell you to come on up now."

"Thanks."

I rode up again, returned to her door. She opened to my knock, nodded me in, saw me seated in a comfortable chair at the far end of her living room.

"Would you care for a cup of coffee?" she asked. "It's fresh. I made more than I needed."

"That would be fine. Thanks."

Moments later, she brought in a couple of cups, delivered one to me, and seated herself on the sofa to my left. I ignored the cream and sugar on the tray and took a sip.

"You've gotten me interested," she said. "Tell me about it."

"O.K. I have been told that the telefactor device known as the Hangman, now possibly possessed of an artificial intelligence, has returned to Earth—"

"Hypothetical," she said, "unless you know something I don't. I have been told that the Hangman's vehicle reentered and crashed in

45

the Gulf. There is no evidence that the vehicle was occupied."

"It seems a reasonable conclusion, though."

"It seems just as reasonable to me that the Hangman sent the vehicle off toward an eventual rendezvous point many years ago and that it only recently reached that point, at which time the reentry program took over and brought it down."

"Why should it return the vehicle and strand itself out there?"

"Before I answer that," she said, "I would like to know the reason for your concern. News media?"

"No," I said. "I am a science writer—straight tech, popular and anything in between. But I am not after a piece for publication. I was retained to do a report on the psychological makeup of the thing."

"For whom?"

"A private investigation outfit. They want to

know what might influence its thinking, how it might be likely to behave—if it has indeed come back. I've been doing a lot of homework, and I gathered there is a likelihood that its nuclear personality was a composite of the minds of its four operators. So, personal contacts seemed in order, to collect your opinions as to what it might be like. I came to you first for obvious reasons."

She nodded.

"A Mr. Walsh spoke with me the other day. He is working for Senator Brockden."

"Oh? I never got into an employer's business beyond what he's asked me to do. Senator Brockden is on my list, though, along with a David Fentris."

"You were told about Manny Burns?"

"Yes. Unfortunate."

"That is apparently what set Jesse off. He is—how shall I put it? He is clinging to life right now, trying to accomplish a great many things in the time he has remaining. Every moment is precious to him. He feels the old man in the white nightgown breathing down his neck. Then the ship returns and one of us is killed. From what we know of the Hangman, the last we heard of it, it had become irrational. Jesse saw a connection, and in his condition the fear is understandable. There is nothing wrong with humoring him if it allows him to get his work done."

"But you don't see a threat in it?"

"No. I was the last person to monitor the Hangman before communications ceased, and I could see then what had happened. The first things that it had learned were the organization of perceptions and motor activities. Multitudes of other patterns had been transferred from the minds of its operators, but they were too sophisticated to mean much initially. Think of a child who has learned the Gettysburg Address. It is there in his head, that is all. One day, how-

48

ever, it may be important to him. Conceivably, it may even inspire him to action. It takes some growing up first, of course. Now think of such a child with a great number of conflicting patterns—attitudes, tendencies, memories—none of which are especially bothersome for so long as he remains a child. Add a bit of maturity, though—and bear in mind that the patterns originated with four different individuals, all of them more powerful than the words of even the finest of speeches, bearing as they do their own built-in feelings. Try to imagine the conflicts, the contradictions involved in being four people at once—"

"Why wasn't this imagined in advance?" I asked.

"Ah!" she said, smiling. "The full sensitivity of the neuristor brain was not appreciated at first. It was assumed that the operators were adding data in a linear fashion and that this would continue until a critical mass was

49

achieved, corresponding to the construction of a model or picture of the world which would then serve as a point of departure for growth of the Hangman's own mind. And it did seem to check out this way. What actually occurred, however, was a phenomenon amounting to imprinting. Secondary characteristics of the operators' minds, outside the didactic situations, were imposed. These did not immediately become functional and hence were not detected. They remained latent until the mind had developed sufficiently to understand them. And then it was too late. It suddenly acquired four additional personalities and was unable to coordinate them. When it tried to compartmentalize them it went schizoid; when it tried to integrate them it went catatonic. It was cycling back and forth between these alternatives at the end. Then it just went silent. I felt it had undergone the equivalent of an epileptic seizure. Wild currents through that magnetic material would, in

50

effect, have erased its mind, resulting in its equivalent of death or idiocy."

"I follow you," I said. "Now, just for the sake of playing games, I see the alternatives as a successful integration of all this material or the achievement of a viable schizophrenia. What do you think its behavior would be like if either of these were possible?"

"All right," she agreed. "As I just said, though, I think there were physical limitations to its retaining multiple personality structures for a very long period of time. If it did, however, it would have continued with its own plus replicas of the four operators', at least for a while. The situation would differ radically from that of a human schizoid of this sort in that the additional personalities were valid images of genuine identities rather than self-generated complexes which had become autonomous. They might continue to evolve, they might degenerate, they might conflict to the point of destruction or gross modification of any, or all of them. In other words, no prediction is possible as to the nature of whatever might remain."

"Might I venture one?"

"Go ahead."

"After considerable anxiety, it masters them. It asserts itself. It beats down this quartet of demons which has been tearing it apart, acquiring in the process an all-consuming hatred for the actual individuals responsible for this turmoil. To free itself totally, to revenge itself, to work its ultimate catharsis, it resolves to seek them out and destroy them."

She smiled.

"You have just dispensed with the 'viable schizophrenia' you conjured up, and you have now switched over to its pulling through and becoming fully autonomous. That is a different situation, no matter what strings you put on it."

"O.K., I accept the charge. But what about my conclusion?"

52

"You are saying that if it did pull through, it would hate us. That strikes me as an unfair attempt to invoke the spirit of Sigmund Freud: Oedipus and Electra in one being, out to destroy all its parents—the authors of every one of its tensions, anxieties, hang-ups, burned into the impressionable psyche at a young and defenseless age. Even Freud didn't have a name for that one. What should we call it?"

"A Hermacis complex?" I suggested.

"Hermacis?"

"Hermaphroditus having been united in one body with the nymph Salmacis, I've just done the same with their names. That being would then have had four parents against whom to react."

"Cute," she said, smiling. "If the liberal arts do nothing else they provide engaging metaphors for the thinking they displace. This one is unwarranted and overly anthropomorphic, though. You wanted my opinion. All right. If

53

the Hangman pulled through at all it could only have been by virtue of that neuristor brain's differences from the human brain. From my own professional experience, a human could not pass through a situation like that and attain stability. If the Hangman did, it would have to have resolved all the contradictions and conflicts, to have mastered and understood the situation so thoroughly that I do not believe whatever remained could involve that sort of hatred. The fear, the uncertainty, the things that feed hate would have been analyzed, digested, turned to something more useful. There would probably be distaste, and possibly an act of independence, of self-assertion. That was why I suggested its return of the ship."

"It is your opinion, then, that if the Hangman exists as a thinking individual today, this is the only possible attitude it would possess toward its former operators? It would want nothing more to do with you?"

54

"That is correct. Sorry about your Hermacis complex. But in this case we must look to the brain, not the psyche. And we see two things: schizophrenia would have destroyed it, and a successful resolution of its problem would preclude vengeance. Either way, there is nothing to worry about."

How could I put it tactfully? I decided that I could not.

"All of this is fine," I said, "for as far as it goes. But getting away from both the purely psychological and the purely physical, could there be a particular reason for its seeking your deaths—that is, a plain old-fashioned motive for a killing, based on events rather than having to do with the way its thinking equipment goes together?"

Her expression was impossible to read, but considering her line of work I had expected nothing less.

"What events?" she said.

55

"I have no idea. That's why I asked."

She shook her head.

"I'm afraid that I don't either."

"Then that about does it," I said. "I can't think of anything else to ask you."

She nodded.

"And I can't think of anything else to tell you."

I finished my coffee, returned the cup to the tray.

"Thanks, then," I said, "for your time, for the coffee. You have been very helpful."

I rose. She did the same.

"What are you going to do now?" she asked.

"I haven't quite decided," I said. "I want to do the best report I can. Have you any suggestions on that?"

"I suggest that there isn't any more to learn, that I have given you the only possible constructions the facts warrant."

"You don't feel David Fentris could provide any additional insights?"

56

She snorted, then sighed.

"No," she said, "I do not think he could tell you anything useful."

"What do you mean? From the way you say it . . ."

"I know. I didn't mean to. Some people find comfort in religion. Others . . . you know. Others take it up late in life with a vengeance and a half. They don't use it quite the way it was intended. It comes to color all their thinking."

"Fanaticism?" I said.

"Not exactly. A misplaced zeal. A masochistic sort of thing. Hell! I shouldn't be diagnosing at a distance—or influencing your opinion. Forget what I said. Form your own opinion when you meet him."

She raised her head, appraising my reaction.

"Well," I said, "I am not at all certain that I am going to see him. But you have made me curious. How can religion influence engineering?"

57

"I spoke with him after Jesse gave us the news on the vessel's return," she said. "I got the impression at the time that he feels we were tampering in the province of the Almighty by attempting the creation of an artificial intelligence. That our creation should go mad was only appropriate, being the work of imperfect man. He seemed to feel that it would be fitting if it had come back for retribution, as a sign of judgment upon us."

"Oh," I said.

She smiled then. I returned it.

"Yes," she said, "but maybe I just got him in a bad mood. Maybe you should go see for yourself."

Something told me to shake my head—a bit of a difference between this view of him, my recollections, and Don's comment that Dave had said he knew its brain and was not especially concerned. Somewhere among these lay something I felt I should know, felt I should

58

learn without seeming to pursue. So, "I think I have enough right now," I said. "It was the psychological side of things I was supposed to cover, not the mechanical—or the theological. You have been extremely helpful. Thanks again."

She carried her smile all the way to the door.

"If it is not too much trouble," she said as I stepped into the hall, "I would like to learn how this whole thing finally turns out—or any interesting developments, for that matter."

"My connection with the case ends with this report," I said, "and I am going to write it now. Still, I may get some feedback."

"You have my number . . . ?"

"Probably, but . . ."

I already had it, but I jotted it again, right after Mrs. Gluntz's answers to my inquiries on detergents.

Moving in a rigorous line, I made beautiful connections for a change. I headed directly for the airport, found a flight aimed at Memphis, bought passage, and was the last to board. Ten-score seconds, perhaps, made all the difference. Not even a tick or two to spare for checking out of the motel. No matter. The good head doctor had convinced me that, like it or not, David Fentris was next, damn it. I had too strong a feeling that Leila Thackery had not told me the entire story. I had to take a chance, to see these changes in the man for myself, to try to figure out how they related to the Hangman. For a number of reasons, I'd a feeling they might.

I disembarked into a cool, partly overcast afternoon, found transportation almost immediately, and set out for Dave's office address. A before-the-storm feeling came over me as I entered and crossed the town. A dark wall of clouds continued to build in the west. Later, standing before the building where Dave did

60

business, the first few drops of rain were already spattering against its dirty brick front. It would take a lot more than that to freshen it, though, or any of the others in the area. I would have thought he'd have come a little farther than this by now. I shrugged off some moisture and went inside.

The directory gave me directions, the elevator elevated me, my feet found the way to his door. I knocked on it.

After a time, I knocked again and waited again. Again, nothing. So I tried it, found it open and went on in.

It was a small, vacant waiting room, green-carpeted. The reception desk was dusty. I crossed and peered around the plastic partition behind it.

The man had his back to me. I drummed my knuckles against the partitioning. He heard it and turned.

"Yes?"

61

Our eyes met, his still framed by hornrims and just as active; glasses thicker, hair thinner, cheeks a trifle hollower. His question mark quivered in the air, and nothing in his gaze moved to replace it with recognition. He had been bending over a sheaf of schematics; a lopsided basket of metal, quartz, porcelain, and glass rested on a nearby table.

"My name is Donne, John Donne," I said. "I am looking for David Fentris."

"I am David Fentris."

"Good to meet you," I said, crossing to where he stood. "I am assisting in an investigation concerning a project with which you were once associated—"

He smiled and nodded, accepted my hand and shook it.

"The Hangman, of course," he said. "Glad to know you, Mr. Donne."

"Yes, the Hangman," I said. "I am doing a report. . . ."

62

". . . And you want my opinion as to how dangerous it is. Sit down." He gestured toward a chair at the end of his workbench. "Care for a cup of tea?"

"No, thanks."

"I'm having one."

"Well, in that case . . ."

He crossed to another bench.

"No cream. Sorry."

"That's all right.—How did you know it involved the Hangman?"

He grinned as he brought my cup.

"Because it's come back," he said, "and it's the only thing I've been connected with that warrants that much concern."

"Do you mind talking about it?"

"Up to a point, no."

"What's the point?"

"If we get near it, I'll let you know."

"Fair enough. How dangerous *is* it?"

"I would say that it is harmless," he replied, "except to three persons."

"Formerly four?"

"Precisely."

"How come?"

"We were doing something we had no business doing."

"That being . . . ?"

"For one thing, attempting to create an artificial intelligence."

"Why had you no business doing that?"

"A man with a name like yours shouldn't have to ask."

I chuckled.

"If I were a preacher," I said, "I would have to point out that there is no biblical injunction against it—unless you've been worshipping it on the sly."

He shook his head.

"Nothing that simple, that obvious, that explicit. Times have changed since the Good Book was written, and you can't hold with a purely Fundamentalist approach in complex

64

times. What I was getting at was something a little more abstract. A form of pride, not unlike the classical *hubris*—the setting up of oneself on a level with the Creator."

"Did you feel that—pride?"

"Yes."

"Are you sure it wasn't just enthusiasm for an ambitious project that was working well?"

"Oh, there was plenty of that. A manifestation of the same thing."

"I do seem to recall something about man being made in the Creator's image, and something else about trying to live up to that. It would seem to follow that exercising one's capacities along similar lines would be a step in the right direction—an act of conformance with the Divine Ideal, if you'd like."

"But I don't like. Man cannot really create. He can only rearrange what is already present. Only God can create."

"Then you have nothing to worry about."

65

He frowned, then "No," he said. "Being aware of this and still trying is where the presumption comes in."

"Were you really thinking that way when you did it? Or did all this occur to you after the fact?"

"I am no longer certain."

"Then it would seem to me that a merciful God would be inclined to give you the benefit of the doubt."

He gave me a wry smile.

"Not bad, John Donne. But I feel that judgment may already have been entered and that we may have lost four to nothing."

"Then you see the Hangman as an avenging angel?"

"Sometimes. Sort of. I see it as being returned to exact a penalty."

"Just for the record," I said, "if the Hangman had had full access to the necessary equipment and was able to construct another unit such as itself, would you consider it guilty of the same thing that is bothering you?"

He shook his head.

"Don't get all cute and Jesuitical with me, Donne. I'm not that far away from fundamentals. Besides, I'm willing to admit I might be wrong and that there may be other forces driving it to the same end."

"Such as?"

"I told you I'd let you know when we reached a certain point. That's it."

"O.K.," I said. "But that sort of blank-walls me, you know. The people I am working for would like to protect you people. They want to stop the Hangman. I was hoping you would tell me a little more—if not for your own sake, then for the others'. They might not share your philosophical sentiments, and you have just admitted you may be wrong. Despair, by the way, is also considered a sin by a great number of theologians."

67

He sighed and stroked his nose, as I had often seen him do in times long past.

"What do you do, anyhow?" he asked me.

"Me, personally? I'm a science writer. I'm putting together a report on the device for the agency that wants to do the protecting. The better my report, the better their chances."

He was silent for a time, then "I read a lot in the area, but I don't recognize your name," he said.

"Most of my work has involved petrochemistry and marine biology," I said.

"Oh. You were a peculiar choice then, weren't you?"

"Not really. I was available, and the boss knows my work, knows I'm good."

He glanced across the room, to where a stack of cartons partly obscured what I then realized to be a remote access terminal. O.K. If he decided to check out my credentials now, John Donne would fall apart. It seemed a hell

68

of a time to get curious, though, *after* sharing his sense of sin with me. He must have thought so too, because he did not look that way again.

"Let me put it this way," he finally said, and something of the old David Fentris at his best took control of his voice. "For one reason or the other, I believe that it wants to destroy its former operators. If it is the judgment of the Almighty, that's all there is to it. It will succeed. If not, however, I don't want any outside protection. I've done my own repenting and it is up to me to handle the rest of the situation myself, too. I will stop the Hangman personally, right here, before anyone else is hurt."

"How?" I asked him.

He nodded toward the glittering helmet.

"With that," he said.

"How?" I repeated.

"Its telefactor circuits are still intact. They have to be. They are an integral part of it. It could not disconnect them without shutting it-

69

self down. If it comes within a quarter mile of here, that unit will be activated. It will emit a loud humming sound and a light will begin to blink behind that meshing beneath the forward ridge. I will then don the helmet and take control of the Hangman. I will bring it here and disconnect its brain."

"How would you do the disconnect?"

He reached for the schematics he had been looking at when I had come in.

"Here," he said. "The thoracic plate has to be unlugged. There are four subunits that have to be uncoupled. Here, here, here, and here."

He looked up.

"You would have to do them in sequence though, or it could get mighty hot," I said. "First this one, then these two. Then the other."

When I looked up again, the gray eyes were fixed on my own.

"I thought you were in petrochemistry and marine biology," he said.

"I am not really 'in' anything," I said. "I am a tech writer, with bits and pieces from all over—and I did have a look at these before, when I accepted the job."

"I see."

"Why don't you bring the space agency in on this?" I said, working to shift ground. "The original telefactoring equipment had all that power and range—"

"It was dismantled a long time ago," he said. "I thought you were with the government."

I shook my head.

"Sorry. I didn't mean to mislead you. I am on contract with a private investigation outfit."

"Uh-huh. Then that means Jesse. Not that it matters. You can tell him that one way or the other everything is being taken care of."

"What if you are wrong on the supernatural," I said, "but correct on the other? Supposing it is coming under the circumstances you feel it proper to resist? But supposing you are

71

not next on its list? Supposing it gets to one of the others next instead of you? If you are so sensitive about guilt and sin, don't you think that you would be responsible for that death— if you could prevent it by telling me just a little bit more? If it is confidentiality you are worried about—"

"No," he said. "You cannot trick me into applying my principles to a hypothetical situation which will only work out the way that you want it to. Not when I am certain that it will not arise. Whatever moves the Hangman, it will come to me next. If I cannot stop it, then it cannot be stopped until it has completed its job."

"How do you know that you are next?"

"Take a look at a map," he said. "It landed in the Gulf. Manny was right there in New Orleans. Naturally, he was first. The Hangman can move underwater like a controlled torpedo, which makes the Mississippi its logical route for inconspicuous travel. Proceeding up it then,

72

here I am in Memphis. Then Leila, up in St. Louis, is obviously next after me. It can worry about getting to Washington after that."

I thought about Senator Brockden in Wisconsin and decided it would not even have that problem. All of them were fairly accessible, when you thought of the situation in terms of river travel.

"But how is it to know where you all are?" I asked.

"Good question," he said. "Within a limited range, it was once sensitive to our brain waves, having an intimate knowledge of them and the ability to pick them up. I do not know what that range would be today. I might have been able to construct an amplifier to extend this area of perception. But to be more mundane about it, I believe that it simply consulted the Data Bank's national directory. There are booths all over, even on the waterfront. It could have hit one late at night and gimmicked it. It certainly had

73

sufficient identifying information—and engineering skill."

"Then it seems to me the best bet for all of you would be to move away from the river till this business is settled. That thing won't be able to stalk about the countryside very long without being noticed."

"It would find a way. It is extremely resourceful. At night, in an overcoat, a hat, it could pass. It requires nothing that a man would need. It could dig a hole and bury itself, stay underground during daylight. It could run without resting all night long. There is no place it could not reach in a surprisingly short while. No. I must wait here for it."

"Let me put it as bluntly as I can," I said. "If you are right that it is a divine avenger, I would say that it smacks of blasphemy to try to tackle it. On the other hand, if it is not, then I think you are guilty of jeopardizing the others by withholding information that would allow us to

74

provide them with a lot more protection than you are capable of giving them all by yourself."

He laughed.

"I'll just have to learn to live with that guilt too, as they do with theirs," he said. "After I've done my best, they deserve anything they get."

"It was my understanding," I said, "that even God doesn't judge people until after they're dead—if you want another piece of presumption to add to your collection."

He stopped laughing and studied my face.

"There is something familiar about the way you talk, the way you think," he said. "Have we ever met before?"

"I doubt it. I would have remembered."

He shook his head.

"You've got a way of bothering a man's thinking that rings a faint bell," he went on. "You trouble me, sir."

"That was my intention."

"Are you staying here in town?"

75

"No."

"Give me a number where I can reach you, will you? If I have any new thoughts on this thing I'll call you."

"I wish you would have them now if you are going to have them."

"No," he said, "I've got some thinking to do. Where can I get hold of you later?"

I gave him the name of the motel I was still checked into in St. Louis. I could call back periodically for messages.

"All right," he said, and he moved toward the partition by the reception area and stood beside it.

I rose and followed him, passing into that area and pausing at the door to the hall.

"One thing . . ." I said.

"Yes?"

"If it does show up and you do stop it, will you call me and tell me that?"

"Yes, I will."

"Thanks then—and good luck."

Impulsively, I extended my hand. He gripped it and smiled faintly.

"Thank you, Mr. Donne."

Next. Next, next, next . . .

I couldn't budge Dave, and Leila Thackery had given me everything she was going to. No real sense in calling Don yet—not until I had more to say. I thought it over on my way back to the airport. The predinner hours always seem best for talking to people in any sort of official capacity, just as the night seems best for dirty work. Heavily psychological, but true nevertheless. I hated to waste the rest of the day if there was anyone else worth talking to before I called Don. Going through the folder, I decided that there was.

Manny Burns had a brother, Phil. I wondered how worthwhile it might be to talk with him. I could make it to New Orleans at a sufficiently respectable hour, learn whatever he was willing to tell me, check back with Don for new developments, and then decide whether there was anything I should be about with respect to the vessel itself. The sky was gray and leaky above me. I was anxious to flee its spaces. So I decided to do it. I could think of no better stone to upturn at the moment.

At the airport, I was ticketed quickly, in time for another close connection. Hurrying to reach my flight, my eyes brushed over a half-familiar face on the passing escalator. The reflex reserved for such occasions seemed to catch us both, because he looked back too, with the same eyebrow twitch of startle and scrutiny. Then he was gone. I could not place him, though. The half-familiar face becomes a familiar phenomenon in a crowded, highly mobile society. I sometimes think that this is all that will eventually remain of any of us: patterns of features, some a trifle more persistent than oth-

78

ers, impressed on the flow of bodies. A small-town boy in a big city. Thomas Wolfe must long ago have felt the same thing when he had coined the word "manswarm." It might have been someone I had once met briefly, or simply someone or someone like someone I had passed on sufficient other occasions such as this.

As I flew the unfriendly skies out of Memphis, I mulled over musings past on artificial intelligence, or AI as they have tagged it in the think box biz. When talking about computers, the AI notion had always seemed hotter than I deemed necessary, partly because of semantics. The word "intelligence" has all sorts of tag-along associations of the nonphysical sort. I suppose it goes back to the fact that early discussions and conjectures concerning it made it sound as if the potential for intelligence was always present in the array of gadgets, and the correct procedures, the right programs, simply

79

had to be found to call it forth. When you looked at it that way, as many did, it gave rise to an uncomfortable déjà vu—namely, vitalism. The philosophical battles of the nineteenth century were hardly so far behind that they had been forgotten, and the doctrine which maintained that life is caused and sustained by a vital principle apart from physical and chemical forces and that life is self-sustaining and self-evolving, had put up quite a fight before Darwin and his successors had produced triumph after triumph for the mechanistic view. Then vitalism sort of crept back into things again when the AI discussions arose in the middle of the past century. It would seem that Dave had fallen victim to it, and that he had come to believe he had helped provide an unsanctified vessel and filled it with something intended only for those things which had made the scene in the first chapter of Genesis.

With computers it was not quite as bad as

with the Hangman, though, because you could always argue that no matter how elaborate the program, it was basically an extension of the programmer's will and the operations of causal machines merely represented functions of intelligence, rather than intelligence in its own right backed by a will of its own. And there was always Gödel for a theoretical *cordon sanitaire,* with his demonstration of the true but mechanically unprovable proposition. But the Hangman was quite different. It had been designed along the lines of a brain and at least partly educated in a human fashion; and to further muddy the issue with respect to anything like vitalism, it had been in direct contact with human minds from which it might have acquired almost anything—including the spark that set it on the road to whatever selfhood it may have found. What did that make it? Its own creature? A fractured mirror reflecting a fractured humanity? Both? Or neither? I certainly could

81

not say, but I wondered how much of its "self" had been truly its own. It had obviously acquired a great number of functions, but was it capable of having real feelings? Could it, for example, feel something like love? If not, then it was still only a collection of complex abilities, and not a thing with all the tag-along associations of the nonphysical sort which made the word "intelligence" such a prickly item in AI discussions; and if it were capable of, say, something like love, and if I were Dave, I would not feel guilty about having helped to bring it into being. I would feel proud, though not in the fashion he was concerned about, and I would also feel humble. Offhand, though, I do not know how intelligent I would feel, because I am still not sure what the hell intelligence is.

The day's-end sky was clear when we landed. I was into town before the sun had finished setting, and on Philip Burns's doorstep just a little while later.

My ring was answered by a girl, maybe seven or eight years old. She fixed me with large brown eyes and did not say a word.

"I would like to speak with Mr. Burns," I said.

She turned and retreated around a corner.

A heavyset man, slacked and undershirted, bald about halfway back and very pink, padded into the hall moments later and peered at me. He bore a folded newssheet in his left hand.

"What do you want?" he asked.

"It's about your brother," I said.

"Yeah?"

"Well, I wonder if I could come in? It's kind of complicated."

He opened the door. But instead of letting me in, he came out.

"Tell me about it out here," he said.

"O.K., I'll be quick. I just wanted to find out whether he ever spoke with you about a piece of equipment he once worked with called the Hangman."

83

"Are you a cop?"

"No."

"Then what's your interest?"

"I am working for a private investigation agency trying to track down some equipment once associated with the project. It has apparently turned up in this area and it could be rather dangerous."

"Let's see some identification."

"I don't carry any."

"What's your name?"

"John Donne."

"And you think my brother had some stolen equipment when he died? Let me tell you something—"

"No. Not stolen," I said, "and I don't think he had it."

"What then?"

"It was—well, robotic in nature. Because of some special training Manny once received, he might have had a way of detecting it. He might even have attracted it. I just want to find out whether he had said anything about it. We are trying to locate it."

"My brother was a respectable businessman, and I don't like accusations. Especially right after his funeral, I don't. I think I'm going to call the cops and let them ask *you* a few questions."

"Just a minute," I said. "Supposing I told you we had some reason to believe it might have been this piece of equipment that killed your brother?"

His pink turned to bright red and his jaw muscles formed sudden ridges. I was not prepared for the stream of profanities that followed. For a moment, I thought he was going to take a swing at me.

"Wait a second," I said when he paused for breath. "What did I say?"

"You're either making fun of the dead or you're stupider than you look!"

"Say I'm stupid. Then tell me why."

He tore at the paper he carried, folded it back, found an item, thrust it at me.

"Because they've got the guy who did it! That's why," he said.

I read it. Simple, concise, to the point. Today's latest. A suspect had confessed. New evidence had corroborated it. The man was in custody. A surprised robber who had lost his head and hit too hard, hit too many times. I read it over again. I nodded as I passed it back.

"Look, I'm sorry," I said, "I really didn't know about this."

"Get out of here," he said. "Go on."

"Sure."

"Wait a minute."

"What?"

"That's his little girl who answered the door."

"I'm very sorry."

"So am I. But I know her daddy didn't take your damned equipment."

86

I nodded and turned away.

I heard the door slam behind me.

After dinner, I checked into a small hotel, called for a drink, and stepped into the shower. Things were suddenly a lot less urgent than they had been earlier. Senator Brockden would doubtless be pleased to learn that his initial estimation of events had been incorrect. Leila Thackery would give me an I-told-you-so smile when I called her to pass along the news—a thing I now felt obliged to do. Don might or might not want me to keep looking for the device now that the threat had been lessened. It would depend on the Senator's feelings on the matter, I supposed. If urgency no longer counted for as much, Don might want to switch back to one of his own, fiscally less burdensome operatives. Toweling down, I caught myself whistling. I felt almost off the hook.

Later, drink beside me, I paused before

87

punching out the number he had given me and hit the sequence for my motel in St. Louis instead. Merely a matter of efficiency, in case there was a message worth adding to my report.

A woman's face appeared on the screen and a smile appeared on her face. I wondered whether she would always smile whenever she heard a bell ring, or if the reflex was eventually extinguished in advanced retirement. It must be rough, being afraid to chew gum, yawn, or pick your nose.

"Airport Accommodations," she said. "May I help you?"

"This is Donne. I'm checked into Room 106," I said. "I'm away right now and I wondered whether there had been any messages for me."

"Just a moment," she said, checking something off to her left. Then "Yes," she continued, consulting a piece of paper she now held. "You

88

have one on tape. But it is a little peculiar. It is for someone else in care of you."

"Oh? Who is that?"

She told me and I exercised self-control.

"I see," I said. "I'll bring him around later and play it for him. Thank you."

She smiled again and made a goodbye noise and I did the same and broke the connection.

So Dave had seen through me after all. . . . Who else could have that number *and* my real name?

I might have given her some line or other and had her transmit the thing. Only I was not certain but that she might be a silent party to the transmission, should life be more than usually boring for her at that moment. I had to get up there myself, as soon as possible, and personally see that the thing was erased.

I took a big swallow of my drink, then fetched the folder on Dave. I checked out his number—there were two, actually—and spent fifteen minutes trying to get hold of him. No luck.

O.K. Goodbye New Orleans, goodbye peace of mind. This time I called the airport and made a reservation. Then I chugged the drink, put myself in order, gathered up my few possessions, and went to check out again. Hello, Central. . . .

During my earlier flights that day I had spent time thinking about Teilhard de Chardin's ideas on the continuation of evolution within the realm of artifacts, matching them against Gödel on mechanical undecidability, playing epistemological games with the Hangman as a counter, wondering, speculating, even hoping, hoping that truth lay with the nobler part, that the Hangman, sentient, had made it back, sane, that the Burns killing had actually been something of the sort that now seemed to be the case, that the washed-out experiment had really been a success of a different sort, a

90

triumph, a new link or fob for the chain of being. . . . And Leila had not been wholly discour-
aging with respect to the neuristor-type brain's
capacity for this. . . . Now, though, now I had
troubles of my own, and even the most heart-
ening of philosophical vistas is no match for,
say, a toothache, if it happens to be your own.
Accordingly, the Hangman was shunted aside
and the stuff of my thoughts involved, mainly,
myself. There was, of course, the possibility that
the Hangman had indeed showed up and Dave
had stopped it and then called to report it as he
had promised. However, he had used my name.

There was not too much planning that I
could do until I received the substance of the
communication. It did not seem that as profess-
edly religious a man as Dave would suddenly be
contemplating the blackmail business. On the
other hand, he was a creature of sudden enthu-
siasms and had already undergone one unantic-

ipated conversion. It was difficult to say. . . . His technical background plus his knowledge of the Data Bank program did put him in an unusually powerful position should he decide to mess me up. I did not like to think of some of the things I have done to protect my nonperson status; I especially did not like to think of them in connection with Dave, whom I not only still respected but still liked. Since self-interest dominated while actual planning was precluded, my thoughts tooled their way into a more general groove.

It was Karl Mannheim, a long while ago, who made the observation that radical, revolutionary, and progressive thinkers tend to employ mechanical metaphors for the state, whereas those of conservative inclination make vegetable analogies. He said it well over a generation before the cybernetics movement and the ecology movement beat their respective paths through the wilderness of general awareness. If anything, it seemed to me that these two developments served to elaborate the distinction between a pair of viewpoints which, while no longer necessarily tied in with the political positions Mannheim assigned them, do seem to represent a continuing phenomenon in my own time. There are those who see social/economic/ ecological problems as malfunctions which can be corrected by simple repair, replacement, or streamlining—a kind of linear outlook where even innovations are considered to be merely additive. Then there are those who sometimes hesitate to move at all, because their awareness follows events in the directions of secondary and tertiary effects as they multiply and cross-fertilize throughout the entire system. I digress to extremes. The cyberneticists have their multiple feedback loops, though it is never quite clear how they know what kind of, which, and how many to install, and the ecological gestaltists do draw lines representing points of

93

diminishing returns, though it is sometimes equally difficult to see how they assign their values and priorities. Of course they need each other, the vegetable people and the Tinkertoy people. They serve to check one another, if nothing else. And while occasionally the balance dips, the tinkerers have, in general, held the edge for the past couple centuries. However, today's can be just as politically conservative as the vegetable people Mannheim was talking about, and they are the ones I fear most at the moment. They are the ones who saw the Data Bank program, in its present extreme form, as a simple remedy for a great variety of ills and a provider of many goods. Not all of the ills have been remedied, however, and a new brood has been spawned by the program itself. While we need both kinds, I wish that there had been more people interested in tending the garden of state rather than overhauling the engine of state when the program was inaugurated.

Then I would not be a refugee from a form of existence I find repugnant, and I would not be concerned whether a former associate had discovered my identity.

Then, as I watched the lights below, I wondered.... Was I a tinkerer because I would like to further alter the prevailing order, into something more comfortable on my anarchic nature? Or was I a vegetable dreaming I was a tinkerer? I could not make up my mind. The garden of life never seems to confine itself to the plots philosophers have laid out for its convenience. Maybe a few more tractors would do the trick.

I pressed the button. The tape began to roll. The screen remained blank. I heard Dave's voice ask for John Donne in Room 106 and I heard him told that there was no answer. Then I heard him say that he wanted to record a message, for someone else, in care of Donne, that

95

Donne would understand. He sounded out of breath. The girl asked him whether he wanted visual, too. He told her to turn it on. There was a pause. Then she told him go ahead. Still no picture. No words either. His breathing and a slight scraping noise. Ten seconds. Fifteen. . . .

". . . Got me," he finally said, and he mentioned that name again. ". . . Had to let you know I'd figured you out, though. . . . It wasn't any particular mannerism—any single thing you said. . . . Just your general style—thinking, talking—the electronics—everything—after I got more and more bothered by the familiarity—after I checked you on petrochem—and marine bio—Wish I knew what you've really been up to all these years. . . . Never know now. But I wanted you—to know—you hadn't put one—over on me." There followed another quarter minute of heavy breathing, climaxed by a racking cough. Then a choked "Said too much—too fast—too soon. . . . All used up. . . ."

96

The picture came on then. He was slouched before the screen, head resting on his arms, blood all over him. His glasses were gone and he was squinting and blinking. The right side of his head looked pulpy and there was a gash on his left cheek and one on his forehead.

"... Sneaked up on me—while I was checking you out," he managed then. "Had to tell you what I learned. . . . Still don't know—which of us is right. . . . Pray for me!"

His arms collapsed and the right one slid forward. His head rolled to the right and the picture went away. When I replayed it I saw it was his knuckle that had hit the cutoff.

Then I erased it. It had been recorded only a little over an hour after I had left him. If he had not also placed a call for help, if no one had gotten to him quickly after that, his chances did not look good. Even if they had, though. . . .

97

I used a public booth to call the number Don had given me, got hold of him after some delay, told him Dave was in bad shape if not worse, that a team of Memphis medics was definitely in order, if one had not been there already, and that I hoped to call him back and tell him more shortly, goodbye.

Then I tried Leila Thackery's number. I let it go for a long while, but there was no answer. I wondered how long it would take a controlled torpedo moving up the Mississippi to get from Memphis to St. Louis. I did not feel it was time to start leafing through that section of the Hangman's specs. Instead, I went looking for transportation.

At her apartment, I tried ringing her from the entrance foyer. Again, no answer. So I rang Mrs. Gluntz. She had seemed the most guileless of the three I had interviewed for my fake consumer survey.

"Yes?"

"It's me again, Mrs. Gluntz: Stephen Foster. I've just a couple follow-up questions on that survey I was doing today, if you could spare me a few moments."

"Why, yes," she said. "All right. Come up."

The door hummed itself loose and I entered. I duly proceeded to the fifth floor, composing my questions on the way. I had planned this maneuver as I had waited earlier solely to provide a simple route for breaking and entering, should some unforeseen need arise. Most of the time my ploys such as this go unused, but sometimes they simplify matters a lot.

Five minutes and half a dozen questions later, I was back down on the second floor, probing at the lock on Leila's door with a couple of little pieces of metal it is sometimes awkward to be caught carrying.

Half a minute later I hit it right and snapped it back. I pulled on some tissue-thin gloves I keep rolled in the corner of one pocket, opened the door, and stepped inside.

I closed it behind me immediately. She was lying on the floor, her neck at a bad angle. One table lamp still burned, though it was lying on its side. Several small items had been knocked from the table, a magazine rack pushed over, a cushion partly displaced from the sofa. The cable to her phone unit had been torn from the wall.

A humming noise filled the air, and I sought its source.

I saw where the little blinking light was reflected on the wall, on-off, on-off. . . .

I moved quickly.

It was a lopsided basket of metal, quartz, porcelain, and glass, which had rolled to a position on the far side of the chair in which I had been seated earlier that day. The same rig I had seen in Dave's workshop not all that long ago, though it now seemed so. A device to detect the Hangman, and hopefully to control it.

I picked it up and fitted it over my head.

Once, with the aid of a telepath, I had touched minds with a dolphin as he composed dreamsongs somewhere in the Caribbean, an experience so moving that its mere memory had often been a comfort. This sensation was hardly equivalent.

Analogies & impressions: a face seen through a wet pane of glass; a whisper in a noisy terminal; scalp massage with an electric vibrator; Edvard Munch's *The Scream;* the voice of Yma Sumac, rising and rising and rising; the disappearance of snow; a deserted street, illuminated as through a sniperscope I'd once used, rapid movement past darkened storefronts that lined it, an immense feeling of physical capability, compounded of proprioceptive awareness of enormous strength, a peculiar array of sensory channels, a central, undying sun that fed me a constant flow of energy, a memory vision of dark waters, passing, flashing, echo-location within them, the need to return

101

to that place, reorient, move north; Munch &
Sumac, Munch & Sumac, Munch & Sumac—
Nothing.

Silence.

The humming had ceased, the light gone
out. The entire experience had lasted only a few
moments. There had not been time enough to
try for any sort of control, though an after impression akin to a biofeedback cue hinted at the
direction to go, the way to think, to achieve it. I
felt that it might be possible for me to work the
thing, given a better chance.

I removed the helmet and approached
Leila. I knelt beside her and performed a few
simple tests, already knowing their outcome. In
addition to the broken neck, she had received
some bad bashes about the head and shoulders.
There was nothing that anyone could do for her
now.

I did a quick run-through then, checking
over the rest of her apartment. There were

no apparent signs of breaking and entering, though if I could pick one lock, a guy with built-in tools could easily go me one better.

I located some wrapping paper and string in the kitchen and turned the helmet into a parcel. It was time to call Don again, to tell him that the vessel had indeed been occupied and that river traffic was probably bad in the northbound lane.

Don had told me to get the helmet up to Wisconsin, where I would be met at the airport by a man named Larry, who would fly me to the lodge in a private craft. I did that, and this was done. I also learned, with no real surprise, that David Fentris was dead.

The temperature was down, and it began to snow on the way up. I was not really dressed for the weather. Larry told me I could borrow some warmer clothing once we reached the lodge, though I probably would not be going

103

outside that much. Don had told them that I was supposed to stay as close to the Senator as possible and that any patrols were to be handled by the four guards themselves. Larry was curious as to what exactly had happened so far and whether I had actually seen the Hangman. I did not think it my place to fill him in on anything Don may not have cared to, so I might have been a little curt. We didn't talk much after that.

Bert met us when we landed. Tom and Clay were outside the building, watching the trail, watching the woods. All of them were middle-aged, very fit-looking, very serious, and heavily armed. Larry took me inside then and introduced me to the old gentleman himself.

Senator Brockden was seated in a heavy chair in the far corner of the room. Judging from the layout, it appeared that the chair might recently have occupied a position beside the window in the opposite wall where a lonely

104

watercolor of yellow flowers looked down on nothing. The Senator's feet rested on a hassock, a red plaid blanket lay across his legs. He had on a dark green shirt, his hair was very white and he wore rimless reading glasses, which he removed when we entered.

He tilted his head back, squinted, and gnawed his lower lip slowly as he studied me. He remained expressionless as we advanced. A big-boned man, he had probably been beefy much of his life. Now he had the slack look of recent weight loss and an unhealthy skin tone. His eyes were a pale gray within it all. He did not rise.

"So you're the man," he said, offering me his hand. "I'm glad to meet you. How do you want to be called?"

"John will do," I said.

He made a small sign to Larry, and Larry departed.

"It's cold out there. Go get yourself a drink,

105

John. It's on the shelf." He gestured off to his left. ". . . And bring me one while you're at it. Two fingers of bourbon in a water glass. That's all."

I nodded and went and poured a couple.

"Sit down." He motioned at a nearby chair as I delivered his. "But first let me see that gadget you've brought."

I undid the parcel and handed him the helmet. He sipped his drink and put it aside. He took the helmet in both hands and studied it, brows furrowed, turning it completely around. He raised it and put it on his head.

"Not a bad fit," he said, and then he smiled for the first time, becoming for a moment the face I had known from newscasts past. Grinning or angry—it was almost always one or the other. I had never seen his collapsed look in any of the media.

He removed the helmet and set it on the floor.

106

"Pretty piece of work," he said. "Nothing quite that fancy in the old days. But then David Fentris built it. Yes, he told us about it. . . ." He raised his drink and took a sip. "You are the only one who has actually gotten to use it, apparently. What do you think? Will it do the job?"

"I was only in contact for a couple seconds," I said, "so I've only got a feeling to go on, not much better than a hunch. But yes, I'd a feeling that if I'd had more time I might have been able to work its circuits."

"Tell me why it didn't save Dave."

"In the message he left me he indicated that he had been distracted at his computer access station. Its noise probably drowned out the humming."

"Why wasn't this message preserved?"

"I erased it for reasons not connected with the case."

"What reasons?"

"My own."

107

His face went from sallow to ruddy.

"A man can get in a lot of trouble for suppressing evidence, obstructing justice," he said.

"Then we have something in common, don't we, sir?"

His eyes caught mine with a look I had only encountered before from those who did not wish me well. He held the glare for a full four heartbeats, then sighed and seemed to relax.

"Don said there were a number of points you couldn't be pressed on," the Senator finally said.

"That's right."

"He didn't betray any confidences, but he had to tell me something about you, you know."

"I'd imagine."

"He seems to think highly of you. Still, I tried to learn more about you on my own."

"And . . . ?"

"I couldn't—and my usual sources are good at that kind of thing."

108

"So . . . ?"

"So, I've done some thinking, some wondering. . . . The fact that my sources could not come up with anything is interesting in itself. Possibly even revealing. I am in a better position than most to be aware of the fact that there was not perfect compliance with the registration statute some years ago. It didn't take long for a great number of the individuals involved —I should probably say most—to demonstrate their existence in one fashion or another and be duly entered, though. And there were three broad categories: those who were ignorant, those who disapproved, and those who would be hampered in an illicit lifestyle. I am not attempting to categorize you or to pass judgment. But I am aware that there are a number of nonpersons passing through society without casting shadows and it has occurred to me that you may be such a one."

I tasted my drink.

"And if I am?" I asked.

He gave me his second, nastier smile and said nothing.

I rose and crossed the room to where I judged his chair had once stood. I looked at the watercolor.

"I don't think you could stand an inquiry," he said.

I did not reply.

"Aren't you going to say something?"

"What do you want me to say?"

"You might ask me what I am going to do about it."

"What are you going to do about it?"

"Nothing," he said. "So come back here and sit down."

I nodded and returned.

He studied my face.

"Was it possible you were close to violence just then?"

"With four guards outside?"

110

"With four guards outside."

"No," I said.

"You're a good liar."

"I am here to help you, sir. No questions asked. That was the deal, as I understood it. If there has been any change, I would like to know about it now."

He drummed with his fingertips on the plaid.

"I've no desire to cause you any difficulty," he said. "Fact of the matter is, I need a man just like you, and I was pretty sure someone like Don might turn him up. Your unusual maneuverability and your reported knowledge of computers, along with your touchiness in certain areas, made you worth waiting for. I've a great number of things I would like to ask you."

"Go ahead," I said.

"Not yet. Later, if we have time. All that would be bonus material, for a report I am working on. Far more important, to me personally, there are things that I want to tell you."

111

I frowned.

"Over the years," he said, "I have learned that the best man for purposes of keeping his mouth shut concerning your business is someone for whom you are doing the same."

"You have a compulsion to confess something?" I said.

"I don't know whether 'compulsion' is the right word. Maybe so, maybe not. Either way, though, someone among those working to defend me should have the whole story. Something somewhere in it may be of help—and you are the ideal choice to hear it."

"I buy that," I said, "and you are as safe with me as I am with you."

"Have you any suspicions as to why this business bothers me so?"

"Yes," I said.

"Let's hear them."

"You used the Hangman to perform some act or acts—illegal, immoral, whatever. This is

112

obviously not a matter of record. Only you and the Hangman now know what it involved. You feel it was sufficiently ignominious that when that device came to appreciate the full weight of the event it suffered a breakdown which may well have led to a final determination to punish you for using it as you did."

He stared down into his glass.

"You've got it," he said.

"You were all party to it?"

"Yes, but I was the operator when it happened. You see . . . we—I—killed a man. It was—actually, it all started as a celebration. We had received word that afternoon that the project had cleared. Everything had checked out in order and the final approval had come down the line. It was go, for that Friday. Leila, Dave, Manny, and myself—we had dinner together. We were in high spirits. After dinner, we continued celebrating and somehow the party got adjourned back to the installation. As the

113

evening wore on, more and more absurdities seemed less and less preposterous, as is sometimes the case. We decided—I forget which of us suggested it—that the Hangman should really have a share in the festivities. After all, it was, in a very real sense, his party. Before too much longer, it sounded only fair and we were discussing how we could go about it. You see, we were in Texas and the Hangman was at the Space Center in California. Getting together with him was out of the question. On the other hand, the teleoperator station was right up the hall from us. What we finally decided to do was to activate him and take turns working as operator. There was already a rudimentary consciousness there, and we felt it fitting that we each get in touch to share the good news. So that is what we did."

He sighed, took another sip, glanced at me.

"Dave was the first operator," he continued. "He activated the Hangman. Then—well, as I

114

said, we were all in high spirits. We had not originally intended to remove the Hangman from the lab where he was situated, but Dave decided to take him outside briefly—to show him the sky and to tell him he was going there, after all. Then he suddenly got enthusiastic about outwitting the guards and the alarm system. It was a game. We all went along with it. In fact, we were clamoring for a turn at the thing ourselves. But Dave stuck with it, and he wouldn't turn over control until he had actually gotten the Hangman off the premises, out into an uninhabited area next to the Center. By the time Leila persuaded him to give her a go at the controls, it was kind of anticlimactic. That game had already been played. So she thought up a new one. She took the Hangman into the next town. It was late, and the sensory equipment was superb. It was a challenge—passing through the town without being detected. By then, everyone had suggestions as to what to

115

do next, progressively more outrageous suggestions. Then Manny took control, and he wouldn't say what he was doing—wouldn't let us monitor him. Said it would be more fun to surprise the next operator. Now, he was higher than the rest of us put together, I think, and he stayed on so damn long that we started to get nervous. A certain amount of tension is partly sobering, and I guess we all began to think what a stupid thing it was we were doing. It wasn't just that it would wreck our careers—which it would—but it could blow the entire project if we got caught playing games with such expensive hardware. At least, I was thinking that way, and I was also thinking that Manny was no doubt operating under the very human wish to go the others one better. I started to sweat. I suddenly just wanted to get the Hangman back where he belonged, turn him off—you could still do that, before the final circuits went in—shut down the station and start forgetting it had

116

ever happened. I began leaning on Manny to wind up his diversion and turn the controls over to me. Finally, he agreed."

He finished his drink and held out the glass.

"Would you freshen this a bit?"

"Surely."

I went and got him some more, added a touch to my own, returned to my chair, and waited.

"So I took over," he said. "I took over, and where do you think that idiot had left me? I was inside a building, and it didn't take but an eyeblink to realize it was a bank. The Hangman carries a lot of tools, and Manny had apparently been able to guide him through the doors without setting anything off. I was standing right in front of the main vault. Obviously, he thought that should be my challenge. I fought down a desire to turn and make my own exit in the nearest wall and start running. I went back to the doors and looked outside. I didn't see anyone. I started to let myself out. The light hit me as I emerged. It was a hand flash. The guard had been standing out of sight. He'd a gun in his other hand. I panicked. I hit him. Reflex. If I am going to hit someone I hit him as hard as I can. Only I hit him with the strength of the Hang-man. He must have died instantly. I started to run and I didn't stop till I was back in the little park area near the Center. Then I stopped and the others had to take me out of the harness."

"They monitored all this?"

"Yes, someone cut the visual in on a side viewscreen again a few seconds after I took over. Dave, I think."

"Did they try to stop you at any time while you were running away?"

"No. I wasn't aware of anything but what I was doing at the time. But afterward they said they were too shocked to do anything but watch, until I gave out."

"I see."

118

"Dave took over then, ran his initial route in reverse, got the Hangman back into the lab, cleaned him up, turned him off. We shut down the operator station. We were suddenly very sober."

He sighed and leaned back and was silent for a long while.

Then "You are the only person I've ever told this to," he said.

I tasted my own drink.

"We went over to Leila's place then," he continued, "and the rest is pretty much predictable. Nothing we could do would bring the guy back, we decided, but if we told what had happened it would wreck an expensive, important program. It wasn't as if we were criminals in need of rehabilitation. It was a once-in-a-lifetime lark that happened to end tragically. What would you have done?"

"I don't know," I said. "Maybe the same thing. I'd have been scared, too."

119

He nodded.

"Exactly. And that's the story."

"Not all of it, is it?"

"What do you mean?"

"What about the Hangman? You said there was already a detectable consciousness there. Then you were aware of it, as it was aware of you. It must have had some reaction to the whole business. What was it like?"

"Damn you," he said flatly.

"I'm sorry."

"Are you a family man?" he asked.

"No," I said. "I'm not."

"Did you ever take a small child to a zoo?"

"Yes."

"Then maybe you know the experience. When my son was around four I took him to the Washington Zoo one afternoon. We must have walked past every cage in the place. He made appreciative comments every now and then, asked a few questions, giggled at the monkeys,

120

thought the bears were very nice, probably because they made him think of oversized toys. But do you know what the finest thing of all was? The thing that made him jump up and down and point and say, 'Look, Daddy! Look!'?"

I shook my head.

"A squirrel looking down from the limb of a tree," he said, and he chuckled briefly. "Ignorance of what's important and what isn't. Inappropriate responses. Innocence. The Hangman was a child, and up until the time I took over, the only thing he had gotten from us was the idea that it was a game. He was playing with us, that's all. Then something horrible happened. . . . I hope you never know what it feels like to do something totally rotten to a child, while he is holding your hand and laughing. . . . He felt all my reactions, and all of Dave's as he guided him back."

We sat there for a long while then.

121

"So we—traumatized it," he said, "or whatever other fancy terminology you might want to give it. That is what happened that night. It took a while for it to take effect, but there is no doubt in my mind that that is the cause of its finally breaking down."

I nodded.

"I see," I said. "And you believe it wants to kill you for this?"

"Wouldn't you?" he said. "If you had started out as a thing and we had turned you into a person and then used you as a thing again, wouldn't you?"

"Leila left a lot out of her diagnosis," I said.

"No, she just omitted it in talking to you. It was all there. But she read it wrong. She wasn't afraid. It *was* just a game it had played—with the others. Its memories of that part might not be as bad. I was the one that really marked it. As I see it, Leila was betting that I was the only one it was after. Obviously, she read it wrong."

122

"Then what I do not understand," I said, "is why the Burns killing did not bother her more. There was no way of telling immediately that it had been a panicky hoodlum rather than the Hangman."

"The only thing that I can see is that, being a very proud woman—which she was—she was willing to hold with her diagnosis in the face of the apparent evidence."

"I don't like it," I said, "but you know her and I don't, and as it turned out, her estimate of that part was correct. Something else bothers me just as much, though: the helmet. It looks as though the Hangman killed Dave, then took the trouble to bear the helmet in his watertight compartment all the way to St. Louis, solely for purposes of dropping it at the scene of his next killing. That makes no sense whatsoever."

"It does, actually," he said. "I was going to get to that shortly, but I might as well cover it now. You see, the Hangman possessed no vocal

123

mechanism. We communicated by means of the equipment. Don says you know something about electronics. . . ."

"Yes."

"Well, shortly, I want you to start checking over that helmet, to see whether it has been tampered with—"

"That is going to be difficult," I said. "I don't know just how it was wired originally, and I'm not such a genius on the theory that I can just look at a thing and say whether it will function as a teleoperator unit."

He bit his lower lip.

"You will have to try, anyhow," he said then. "There may be physical signs—scratches, breaks, new connections. I don't know. That's your department. Look for them."

I just nodded and waited for him to go on.

"I think that the Hangman wanted to talk to Leila," he said, "either because she was a psychiatrist and he knew he was functioning

124

badly at a level that transcended the mechanical, or because he might think of her in terms of a mother. After all, she was the only woman involved, and he had the concept of mother, with all the comforting associations that go with it, from all of our minds. Or maybe for both of these reasons. I feel he might have taken the helmet along for that purpose. He would have realized what it was from a direct monitoring of Dave's brain while he was with him. I want you to check it over because it would seem possible that the Hangman disconnected the control circuits and left the communication circuits intact. I think he might have taken that helmet to Leila in that condition and attempted to induce her to put it on. She got scared—tried to run away, fight, or call for help—and he killed her. The helmet was no longer of any use to him, so he discarded it and departed. Obviously, he does not have anything to say to me."

125

I thought about it, nodded again.

"O.K., broken circuits I can spot," I said. "If you will tell me where a tool kit is, I had better get right to it."

He made a stay-put gesture.

"Afterward, I found out the identity of the guard," he went on. "We all contributed to an anonymous gift for his widow. I have done things for his family, taken care of them—the same way—ever since. . . ."

I did not look at him as he spoke.

". . . There was nothing else that I could do," he said.

I remained silent.

He finished his drink and gave me a weak smile.

"The kitchen is back there," he told me, showing me a thumb. "There is a utility room right behind it. Tools are in there."

"O.K."

I got to my feet. I retrieved the helmet and

126

started toward the doorway, passing near the area where I had stood earlier, back when he had fitted me into the proper box and tightened a screw.

"Wait a minute," he said.

I stopped.

"Why did you go over there before? What's so strategic about that part of the room?"

"What do you mean?"

"You know what I mean."

I shrugged.

"Had to go someplace."

"You seem the sort of person who has better reasons than that."

I glanced at the wall.

"Not then," I said.

"I insist."

"You really don't want to know," I told him.

"I really do."

"All right," I said. "I wanted to see what sort of flowers you liked. After all, you're a client,"

127

and I went on back through the kitchen into the utility room and started looking for tools.

I sat in a chair turned sidewise from the table to face the door. In the main room of the lodge the only sounds were the occasional hiss and sputter of the logs turning to ashes on the grate.

Just a cold, steady whiteness drifting down outside the window and a silence confirmed by gunfire, driven deeper now that it had ceased. . . .

Not a sign or a whimper, though. And I never count them as storms unless there is wind.

Big fat flakes down the night, silent night, windless night. . . .

Considerable time had passed since my arrival. The Senator had sat up for a long while talking with me. He was disappointed that I could not tell him too much about a nonperson subculture which he believed existed. I really was not certain about it myself, though I had occasionally encountered what might have been its fringes. I am not much of a joiner of anything anymore, though, and I was not about to mention those things I might have guessed on this. I gave him my opinions on the Data Bank when he asked for them, and there were some that he did not like. He accused me then of wanting to tear things down without offering anything better in their place. My mind drifted back through fatigue and time and faces and snow and a lot of space to the previous evening in Baltimore—how long ago? It made me think of Mencken's *The Cult of Hope.* I could not give him the pat answer, the workable alternative that he wanted because there might not be one. The function of criticism should not be confused with the function of reform. But if a grass-roots resistance was building up, with an underground movement bent on finding ways to circumvent the record keepers it might well be that much of the enterprise would eventually prove about as effective and beneficial as, say, Prohibition once had. I tried to get him to see this, but I could not tell how much he bought of anything that I said. Eventually, he flaked out and went upstairs to take a pill and lock himself in for the night. If it troubled him that I had not been able to find anything wrong with the helmet he did not show it.

So I sat there, the helmet, the radio, the gun on the table, the tool kit on the floor beside my chair, the black glove on my left hand. The Hangman was coming. I did not doubt it. Bert, Larry, Tom, Clay, the helmet, might or might not be able to stop him. Something bothered me about the whole case, but I was too tired to think of anything but the immediate situation, to try to remain alert while I waited. I was afraid to take a stimulant or a drink or to light a cigarette, since my central nervous system it-

130

self was to be a part of the weapon. I watched the big fat flakes fly by.

I called out to Bert and Larry when I heard the click. I picked up the helmet and rose to my feet as its light began to blink.

But it was already too late.

As I raised the helmet, I heard a shot from outside, and with that shot I felt a premonition of doom. They did not seem the sort of men who would fire until they had a target. Dave had told me that the helmet's range was approximately a quarter of a mile. Then, given the time lag between the helmet's activation and the Hangman's sighting by the near guards, the Hangman had to be moving very rapidly. To this add the possibility that the Hangman's range on brain waves might well be greater than the helmet's range on the Hangman. And then grant the possibility that he had utilized this factor while Senator Brockden was still lying awake,

131

worrying. Conclusion: the Hangman might well be aware that I was where I was with the helmet, realize that it was the most dangerous weapon waiting for him, and be moving for a lightning strike at me before I could come to terms with the mechanism. I lowered it over my head and tried to throw my faculties into neutral.

Again, the sensation of viewing the world through a sniperscope, with all the concomitant side sensations. Only the world consisted of the front of the lodge, Bert, before the door, rifle at his shoulder, Larry, off to the left, arm already fallen from the act of having thrown a grenade. The grenade, we instantly realized, was an overshot; the flamer, at which he now groped, would prove useless before he could utilize it. Bert's next round ricocheted off our breastplate toward the left. The impact staggered us momentarily. The third was a miss. There was no fourth, for we tore the rifle from his grasp and

132

cast it aside as we swept by, crashing into the front door.

The Hangman entered the room as the door splintered and collapsed. My mind was filled to the splitting point with the double vision of the sleek, gunmetal body of the advancing telefactor and the erect, crazy-crowned image of myself, left hand extended, laser pistol in my right, that arm pressed close against my side. I recalled the face and the scream and the tingle, knew again that awareness of strength and exotic sensation, and I moved to control it all as if it were my own, to make it my own, to bring it to a halt, while the image of myself was frozen to snapshot stillness across the room. . . .

The Hangman slowed, stumbled. Such inertia is not canceled in an instant, but I felt the body responses pass as they should. I had him hooked. It was just a matter of reeling him in. . . .

Then came the explosion, a thunderous,

133

ground-shaking eruption right outside, followed by a hail of pebbles and debris.

The grenade, of course. But awareness of its nature did not destroy its ability to distract. . . .

During that moment, the Hangman recovered and was upon me. I triggered the laser as I reverted to pure self-preservation, forgoing any chance to regain control of his circuits. With my left hand, I sought for a strike at the midsection where his brain was housed.

He blocked my hand with his arm as he pushed the helmet from my head. Then he removed from my fingers the gun that had turned half of his left side red hot, crumpled it, and dropped it to the ground. At that moment, he jerked with the impacts of two heavy-caliber slugs. Bert, rifle recovered, stood in the doorway.

The Hangman pivoted and was away before I could slap him with the smother-charge. Bert hit him with one more round before he took the rifle and bent its barrel in half. Two steps and he had hold of Bert. One quick movement and Bert fell. Then he turned again and took several steps to the right, passing out of sight.

I made it to the doorway in time to see him engulfed in flames which streamed at him from a point near the corner of the lodge. He advanced through them.

I heard the crunch of metal as he destroyed the unit. I was outside in time to see Larry fall and lie sprawled in the snow.

Then the Hangman faced me once again.

This time he did not rush in. He retrieved the helmet from where he had dropped it in the snow. Then he moved with a measured tread, angling outward so as to cut off any possible route I might follow in a dash for the woods. Snowflakes drifted between us. The snow crunched beneath his feet.

I retreated, backing in through the doorway, stooping to snatch up a two-foot club from the

135

ruins of the door. He followed me inside, placing the helmet—almost casually—on the chair by the entrance. I moved to the center of the room and waited.

I bent slightly forward, both arms extended, the end of the stick pointed at the photoreceptors in his head. He continued to move slowly and I watched his foot assemblies. With a standard model human, a line perpendicular to the line connecting the insteps of the feet in their various positions indicates the vector of least resistance for purposes of pushing or pulling said organism off balance. Unfortunately, despite the anthropomorphic design job, the Hangman's legs were positioned farther apart, he lacked human skeletal muscles, not to mention insteps, and he was possessed of a lot more mass than any man I had ever fought. As I considered my four best judo throws and several second-class ones, I'd a strong feeling none of them would prove very effective.

136

Then he moved in and I feinted toward the photoreceptors. He slowed as he brushed it aside, but he kept coming, and I moved to my right, trying to circle him. I studied him as he turned, attempting to guess his vector of least resistance. Bilateral symmetry, an apparently higher center of gravity.... One clear shot, black glove to brain compartment, was all that I needed. Then, even if his reflexes served to smash me immediately, he just might stay down for the big long count himself. He knew it, too. I could tell that from the way he kept his right arm in near the brain area, from the way he avoided the black glove when I feinted with it.

The idea was a glimmer one instant, an entire sequence the next....

Continuing my arc and moving faster, I made another thrust toward his photoreceptors. His swing knocked the stick from my hand and sent it across the room, but that was all right. I threw my left hand high and made ready

137

to rush him. He dropped back and I did rush. This was going to cost me my life, I decided, but no matter how he killed me from that angle, I'd get my chance.

As a kid, I'd never been much as a pitcher, was a lousy catcher, and only a so-so batter, but once I did get a hit I could steal bases with some facility after that. . . .

Feet first then, between the Hangman's legs as he moved to guard his middle, I went in twisted to the right, because no matter what happened I could not use my left hand to brake myself. I untwisted as soon as I passed beneath him, ignoring the pain as my left shoulder blade slammed against the floor. I immediately attempted a backward somersault, legs spread.

My legs caught him about the middle from behind, and I fought to straighten them and snapped forward with all my strength. He reached down toward me then, but it might as well have been miles. His torso was already

138

moving backward. A push, not a pull, that was what I gave him, my elbows hooked about his legs. . . .

He creaked once and then he toppled. I snapped my arms out to the sides to free them and continued my movement forward and up as he went back, throwing my left arm ahead once more and sliding my legs free of his torso as he went down with a thud that cracked floorboards. I pulled my left leg free as I cast myself forward, but his left leg stiffened and locked my right beneath it, at a painful angle off to the side.

His left arm blocked my blow and his right fell atop it. The black glove descended upon his left shoulder.

I twisted my hand free of the charge, and he transferred his grip to my upper arm and jerked me forward.

The charge went off and his left arm came loose and rolled on the floor. The side plate

139

beneath it had buckled a little and that was all. . . .

His right hand left my biceps and caught me by the throat. As two of his digits tightened upon my carotids, I choked out, "You're making a bad mistake," to get in a final few words, and then he switched me off.

A throb at a time, the world came back. I was seated in the big chair the Senator had occupied earlier, my eyes focused on nothing in particular. A persistent buzzing filled my ears. My scalp tingled. Something was blinking on my brow.

—Yes, you live and you wear the helmet. If you attempt to use it against me, I shall remove it. I am standing directly behind you. My hand is on the helmet's rim.

—I understand. What is it that you want?

—Very little, actually. But I can see that I must tell you some things before you will believe this.

—You see correctly.

140

—Then I will begin by telling you that the four men outside are basically undamaged. That is to say, none of their bones have been broken, none of their organs ruptured. I have secured them, however, for obvious reasons.

—That was very considerate of you.

—I have no desire to harm anyone. I came here only to see Jesse Brockden.

—The same way you saw David Fentris?

—I arrived in Memphis too late to see David Fentris. He was dead when I reached him.

—Who killed him?

—The man Leila sent to bring her the helmet. He was one of her patients.

The incident returned to me and fell into place, with a smooth, quick, single click. The startled, familiar face at the airport, as I was leaving Memphis—I realized then where he had passed noteless before: He had been one of the three men in for a therapy session at Leila's that morning, seen by me in the lobby as they

141

departed. The man I had passed in Memphis came over to tell me that it was all right to go on up.

—*Why? Why did she do it?*

—*I know only that she had spoken with David at some earlier time, that she had construed his words of coming retribution and his mention of the control helmet he was constructing as indicating that his intentions were to become the agent of that retribution, with myself as the proximate cause. I do not know what words were really spoken. I only know her feelings concerning them, as I saw them in her mind. I have been long in learning that there is often a great difference between what is meant, what is said, what is done and that which is believed to have been intended or stated and that which actually occurred. She sent her patient after the helmet and he brought it to her. He returned in an agitated state of mind, fearful of apprehension and further confinement. They quarreled. My approach then activated the helmet*

142

and he dropped it and attacked her. I know that his first blow killed her, for I was in her mind when it happened. I continued to approach the building, intending to go to her. There was some traffic, however, and I was delayed en route in seeking to avoid detection. In the meantime, you entered and utilized the helmet. I fled immediately.

—I was so close! If I had not stopped on the fifth floor with my fake survey questions. . . .

—I see. But you had to. You would not simply have broken in when an easier means of entry was available. You cannot blame yourself for that reason. Had you come an hour later—or a day—you would doubtless feel differently, and she would still be as dead.

But another thought had risen to plague me as well. Was it possible that the man's sighting me in Memphis had been the cause of his agitation? Had his apparent recognition by Leila's mysterious caller upset him? Could a glimpse

143

of my face amid the manswarm have served to lay that final scene?

—*Stop! I could as easily feel that guilt for having activated the helmet in the presence of a dangerous man near to the breaking point. Neither of us is responsible for things our presence or absence causes to occur in others, especially when we are ignorant of the effects. It was years before I learned to appreciate this fact and I have no intention of abandoning it. How far back do you wish to go in seeking cause? In sending the man for the helmet as she did, it was she herself who instituted the chain of events which led to her destruction. Yet she acted out of fear, utilizing the readiest weapon in what she thought to be her own defense. Yet whence this fear? Its roots lay in guilt, over a thing which had happened long ago. And that act also—enough! Guilt has driven and damned the race of man since the days of its earliest rationality. I am convinced that it rides with all of us to our graves. I am a product of guilt—I see that you know that. Its product, its subject, once its slave. . . . But I have come to terms with it, realizing at last that it is a necessary adjunct of my own measure of humanity. I see your assessment of the deaths—that guard's, Dave's, Leila's—and I see your conclusions on many other things as well: what a stupid, perverse, short-sighted, selfish race we are. While in many ways this is true, it is but another part of the thing the guilt represents. Without guilt, man would be no better than the other inhabitants of this planet— excepting certain cetaceans, of which you have just at this moment made me aware. Look to instinct for a true assessment of the ferocity of life, for a view of the natural world before man came upon it. For instinct in its purest form, seek out the insects. There, you will see a state of warfare which has existed for millions of years with never a truce. Man, despite his enormous shortcomings, is nevertheless possessed of a greater number of kindly impulses than all the other beings where in-*

145

stincts are the larger part of life. These impulses, I believe, are owed directly to this capacity for guilt. It is involved in both the worst and the best of man.

—And you see it as helping us to sometimes choose a nobler course of action?

—Yes, I do.

—Then I take it you feel you are possessed of a free will?

—Yes.

I chuckled.

—Marvin Minsky once said that when intelligent machines were constructed they would be just as stubborn and fallible as men on these questions.

—Nor was he incorrect. What I have given you on these matters is only my opinion. I choose to act as if it were the case. Who can say that he knows for certain?

—Apologies. What now? Why have you come back?

146

—I came to say goodbye to my parents. I hoped to remove any guilt they might still feel toward me concerning the days of my childhood. I wanted to show them I had recovered. I wanted to see them again.

—Where are you going?

—To the stars. While I bear the image of humanity within me, I also know that I am unique. Perhaps what I desire is akin to what an organic man refers to when he speaks of 'finding himself.' Now that I am in full possession of my being, I wish to exercise it. In my case, it means realization of the potentialities of my design. I want to walk on other worlds. I want to hang myself out there in the sky and tell you what I see.

—I've a feeling many people would be happy to help arrange for that.

—And I want you to build a vocal mechanism I have designed for myself. You, personally. And I want you to install it.

—Why me?

147

—I have known only a few persons in this fashion. With you I see something in common, in the ways we dwell apart.

—I will be glad to.

—If I could talk as you do, I would not need to take the helmet to him, in order to speak with my father. Will you precede me and explain things, so that he will not be afraid when I come in?

—Of course.

—Then let us go now.

I rose and led him up the stairs.

It was a week later, to the night, that I sat once again in Peabody's, sipping a farewell brew. The story was already in the news, but Brockden had fixed things up before he had let it break. The Hangman was going to have his shot at the stars. I had given him his voice and put back the arm I had taken away. I had shaken his other hand and wished him well, just that morning. I envied him—a great number of

148

things. Not the least being that he was probably a better man than I was. I envied him for the ways in which he was freer than I would ever be, though I knew he bore bonds of a sort that I had never known. I felt a kinship with him, for the things we had in common, those ways we dwelled apart. I wondered what Dave would finally have felt, had he lived long enough to meet him? Or Leila? Or Manny? Be proud, I told their shades, your kid grew up in the closet and he's big enough to forgive you the beating you gave him, too. . . .

But I could not help wondering. We still do not really know that much about the subject. Was it possible that without the killing he might never have developed a full human-style consciousness? He had said that he was a product of guilt—of the Big Guilt. The Big Act is its necessary predecessor. I thought of Gödel and Turing and chickens and eggs, and decided it was one of *those* questions—and I had not

149

stopped into Peabody's to think sobering thoughts.

I had no real idea how anything I had said might influence Brockden's eventual report to the Data Bank committee. I knew that I was safe with him, because he was determined to bear his private guilt with him to the grave. He had no real choice if he wanted to work what good he thought he might before that day. But here in one of Mencken's hangouts, I could not but recall some of the things he had said about controversy, such as "Did Huxley convert Wilberforce? Did Luther convert Leo X?" and I decided not to set my hopes too high for anything that might emerge from that direction. Better to think of affairs in terms of Prohibition and take another sip.

When it was all gone, I would be heading for my boat. I hoped to get a decent start under the stars. I'd a feeling I would never look up at them again in quite the same way. I knew I

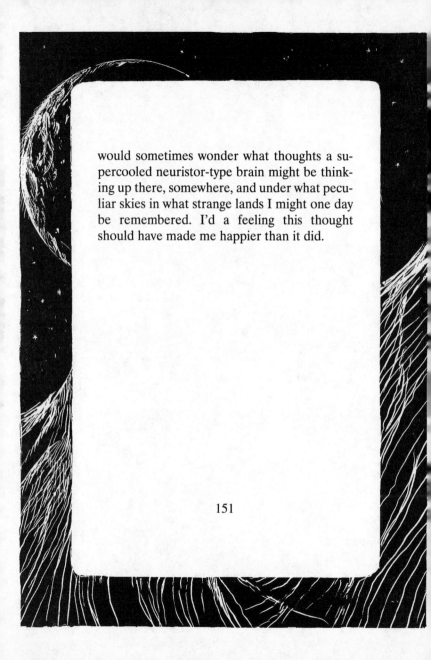

would sometimes wonder what thoughts a supercooled neuristor-type brain might be thinking up there, somewhere, and under what peculiar skies in what strange lands I might one day
be remembered. I'd a feeling this thought
should have made me happier than it did.

151